About The Author

Sue Grainger is a wife, the mother of two adults (at least, that's what the law calls them – but they're fighting it), and has lived in East Yorkshire, England, for her entire life. It's an area she's proud to call 'home'.

Naturally creative, she's an author, an artist, and enjoys baking and decorating cakes for her family and friends. She's also a keen observer of the world around her, and has a passion for music that ranges from classical, to country, to rock.

The stories she writes are a mesh of ideas generated by who she is and who she imagines herself being as part of the plot. The world is a fascinating place, and the people she meets a constant source of inspiration. There are so many talented people out there, so many lifestyles, and so many points of view…

For more information about Sue and her alter-ego Alina Voyce please visit her website:

www.alinavoyce.com

Also by Sue Grainger

The Lifelight Series
(written under pseudonym Alina Voyce):

Hunting Light
Lifelights
Light Evolution
21st Century Light
Chemical Light

Betty Sue's Teatime Tales

Sue Grainger

LIFELIGHT PUBLISHING

Published by Lifelight Publishing 2015
www.lifelightpublishing.com

Cover and Book design by Grainger Graphics

Copyright © 2015 by Sue Grainger
www.alinavoyce.com

British Library Cataloguing in Publication Data.
A catalogue record for the paperback edition of book is
available from the British Library.

ISBN: 978-0-9571817-7-9

1 3 5 7 9 10 8 6 4 2

Table of Contents

In Celebration of Betty Neels

and

'Betties' the world over

With Love

From

Betty Sie

x

Betty Sue's

Teatime Tales

Friends And Lovers

Amy's Ant

Mr Carmichael made a final note on the pages in front of him, and turned his attention to the eight-year-old sitting on the opposite side of the desk. Amy Lambert was chewing on her lip, and not meeting his eyes—as if the abused desk, with its deliberately marked wood, was a fascinating piece of art. Glancing down at it, he supposed it was; biro and compass had been used with flair over several years, and he knew for a fact that these same methods had been extended to the plastic chairs, too. The school really needed some new furniture.

"So, Amy..." he began, pulling her attention back to the reason she was here. "I've read the story you handed in last week, and I wanted to go through a few things with you."

"My spellings are bad," she whispered, before going back to the lip biting.

Taken aback that she'd actually spoken, Mr Carmichael took a moment to reply. "Well, yes, but that's something we can work on and fix. There are some things that are harder to teach."

"Harder than spellings?" Amy's tone suggested disbelief, something that apparently banished shyness.

Mr Carmichael nodded. "Yes. But I'm pleased to say, that's not something you have to worry about. Your story has good structure, with a strong beginning, middle and end, your characters are believable, and your plot line imaginative. So, when you think about it… spellings really aren't that bad. They're just something you have to keep working at until you get used to them."

"My Mum says the French are to blame," Amy offered, "and the Germans." Mr Carmichael wondered if he needed to talk with her female parent about international tolerance, and the appreciation of different cultures. "But mainly the French, especially as the Latin probably came from them too."

"I'm sorry… I don't understand," Mr Carmichael confessed. "Why are the French to blame for you getting your spellings wrong?"

Amy gave him a look that plainly wondered how he could be so stupid. "I thought *you'd* know all about it." She shifted on her seat, and stuck her nose in the air before continuing. "The English language is 29% French, 26% German and 29% Latin, with 16% of words coming from other influences; like Greek and Indian—did you know that pyjamas is an Indian word?"

"Actually… yes I did," Mr Carmichael said. "So, your Mum told you that English words are hard to spell because it's a mix of lots of different languages?"

Amy nodded. "Yes. And all those languages have different spellings for the same sounds. Mum says it makes English a 'hot mess'," she paused, as if trying to figure something out. "She calls it eti…etimolo— something."

"Etymology," Mr Carmichael corrected. "It's the study of where words came from and what they mean."

"Mum says it's really cool, because although it means English is *hard*, it also means we're speaking and writing the history of the British Isles. All the people we invaded and all the people who invaded us are still there… in our language."

Mr Carmichael was enchanted by the whole idea. But they weren't there to talk about history.

"Anyway, as fascinating as all this is, Amy, and your Mum is quite right about that…"

"And Auntie Joan…"

"Auntie Joan?"

"Mum's sister. They talk about stuff like that a *lot*."

Mr Carmichael sighed, but graciously amended his statement. "I see. So, as fascinating as your mum and Auntie Joan find the subject of Etymology, that's not what we should be talking about right now."

"But you wanted to tell me how bad I am at spelling… and I'm explaining why it's not my fault. It's the French's fault," Amy said.

"The fault of the French," Mr Carmichael corrected, rubbing his suddenly aching forehead with the palm of one hand, and wondering if he *really* wanted to add grammar to the debate.

"That's what I said," Amy grumbled.

"Now, about this story," Mr Carmichael said, motioning towards the page of none-too-neat writing in front of him. "It's a very good story, imaginative, whimsical, and I like how you've built the character of the Ant. I particularly like this bit here." He pointed to it, moving the page so that Amy could see where he meant. "The Ant's shiny black eyes was sad. Thier needed to be more cushons and more picktures to make her home feel cosy. She wanted to be as cosy and snug as a bug in a rug."

Amy smiled. "I like that bit too. Dad doesn't like cushions..."

Concerned that they were getting off-track again, Mr Carmichael jumped back into the conversation. "You do have some spelling issues though. I've made a list of all the spellings that are wrong, and I want you to take them home with you and practice them every day. See? Their should be There, cushons should be cushions, and picktures should be pictures."

"But cushions doesn't sound like it has an 'i' in it," Amy complained.

"It's a silent 'i'."

"And pick has a kicking 'k', so why doesn't pictures?"

"Because they have different meanings; the word pictures has nothing to do with the word pick, even if they do sound the same."

"Bet that was the French," Amy muttered.

Mr Carmichael sighed, and reached for the dictionary further along his desk. Flicking through the pages, he ran his finger down the entries, until he came to the word he was looking for. "Actually, the word picture comes from Latin... and before you say it, that doesn't automatically mean the French are to blame for that too."

"How do you know it's Latin?" Amy asked.

Mr Carmichael smiled, pleased that here was something he could show her. Turning the dictionary around, he pointed to the letters at the end of the definition for 'picture'. "You see that capital 'L'? That stands for 'Latin', which tells us where the word originally came from. If you look at other words, you'll see a range of different letters. 'F' is for French, 'G' is for German, 'Gk' is for Greek, 'Du' is for Dutch, and so on..."

Amy giggled. "It's *all* double Dutch to me."

Mr Carmichael gave a rather unprofessional snort, which only made her giggle more. "Very funny. I suppose your Mum taught you that saying too? Now, back to your story: you also need to work on your grammar; I'll show you what I mean..."

At the end of the assessment session, Amy packed up her books and pencil case, and started to scrape back her chair. "It's parents evening tonight, so I'll see you later, Amy," Mr Carmichael reminded her. "I'm looking forward to telling your mum how well you're doing. I'll bring your Ant story too, so she can see for herself."

Amy gave him a small smile, adding a shy wave of her hand as she slipped through the classroom doorway. "See you later, Mr Carmichael."

Parents evening was the usual chaotic mix of children, adults, expectations and high emotion. The school was small enough that time-slots weren't necessary, but that meant there was the occasional bottle-neck, where the lines of parents waiting for certain teachers got ridiculously long. In fact, some parents were known to give up entirely and go home without seeing everyone in their child's education team.

Looking across the crowded room, Mr Carmichael began to wonder if Amy and her mother had done just that. To be honest, the thought of going home himself was beginning to feel like a good idea. He only had

Amy left on his list, and if she'd already gone… He rocked his chair back; unaware that he was doing the very thing he'd warned numerous pupils against, only to crash back into an upright position when a voice all but bellowed in his ear.

"Hi, Mr Carmichael!" Amy shouted, competing with the noise in the hall. "Mum couldn't come tonight, because my brother Steve's sick, and Dad's not home from work yet. So Auntie Joan has come with me. She's really looking forward to meeting you, because I told her all about the story I wrote about her and about the etimolo-stuff, and she says you sound like a really cool teacher, and she wishes she'd had someone like you to learn English from at school…"

Mr Carmichael didn't have the heart to stop Amy's enthusiastic rambling. To be honest, he'd stopped listening after 'the story I wrote about her'. So… it had been another spelling mistake? One he'd failed to put on her list? Looking up, he smiled back at the tall, dark haired, undeniably gorgeous woman who was holding Amy's hand. Her shiny, almost-black eyes were looking somewhat bemused, and he found himself in total sympathy. Aunt *not* Ant—he was definitely blaming the French for that one.

Operation Action Man

It started with a wedding dress—two, to be precise. Both were made from white cotton and organza, with romantic, puffed sleeves, and clusters of flowers along the neckline. They were dresses that any bride would be proud to wear.

Amy, the proud owner of one of them, knew that, and she was positive Sindy did too. It was just a pity that the seven-inch-long creation would never fit Amy herself. Not that this stopped her from imagining how the soft fabric would feel against her skin, or how exciting it would be to walk down the aisle towards... oh, never mind. She picked up a small bouquet, which she'd made from loops of thin ribbon, surrounded by tissue, and pushed the matching headdress, with its attached length of net veil, onto Sindy's sleek, black hair. It immediately fell off. She'd need to find a hair-grip.

"Amy? Lizzie's here!" Mum shouted from the bottom of the stairs.

"I'm in my bedroom... send her up!" Amy yelled back.

There was the distant sound of a politely spoken, "Thank you, Mrs L," a burst of hollow thumps as Lizzie ran up the stairs, and then Amy's bedroom door was shoved open, her friend rushing through the gap, with arms full.

From her perch on the window ledge, Amy smiled, and watched as Lizzie climbed up to sit opposite. The contents of her arms were dropped into the space between them. They and Lizzie were slightly damp...

Surprised, Amy looked out the window, and realised that the sky had turned dark-grey, and was spraying the glass with round, heavy droplets. They smacked against the pane and slid down the smooth surface, in a gravity-driven race. And even as she watched, the fast-flowing rivulets increased in number, the rain quickening. It smeared the lines of the view outside, until it became nothing more than blobs of dull colour.

"Hi, Amy. Did you get him?" Lizzie asked.

Amy's attention snapped back to her friend, and she immediately made a *shushing* noise, her eyes going to the still-open door.

"No, not yet—and keep your voice down. If Steve hears you, we're sunk."

"But I thought he was okay with it?"

Amy rolled her eyes. "Well *of course* he isn't! Boys can be really stupid about things like this."

"Steve isn't stupid," Lizzie said, and then blushed an interesting shade of 'fire-engine red' when Amy sent her a look of suspicion.

"Do *like* my brother, Lizzie? I mean, *like* him, like him?"

"*No!*"

"I think you do."

"Do *not!*"

Amy looked at Lizzie's still-red cheeks and smirked, but decided not to torment her any more. "Okay, so you don't like him. Good job—because he really *is* stupid; especially about girls. He says we're all a waste of space—and we smell."

Apparently deciding not to argue the point, Lizzie said nothing and leaned forward to rescue a blonde-haired Sindy doll from the pile of clothes she'd brought with her. The rounded face, with its wide eyes, pink cheeks and perfect, shiny lips, was almost identical to Amy's Sindy, apart from the hair colour. Even the wedding dress, a Christmas present from Amy's mum, was made from the same material. The only difference was the flowers around the neckline—which were blue on Lizzie's, and pink on Amy's.

"Did you finish the bouquet and headdress for her?" Amy asked.

Lizzie shook her head. "I was going to use some of the beads from Mum's craft drawer, but I couldn't get the lid off the tin she keeps them in."

"Couldn't your mum do it for you?"

"She was busy baking buns for the cake stall at school tomorrow, so…" Lizzie let the sentence trail off, reaching into the pile of dolls' clothes, to pick out a pair of pink ballet shoes. Carefully slipping them onto the feet of her Sindy, she experimented with changing the position of the poseable ankle and knee joints. Watching her, Amy didn't suppose that many brides went down the aisle like a ballerina, but she bet it would look cool if they did.

Then Lizzie's words sank in. "Cake stall? What cake stall?" Amy asked.

"The one we got a letter about last week… remember?"

Amy thought for a moment, and then jumped from the window ledge and pulled her school bag out from under her bed. Delving into it, her fingers found and grasped the crumpled body of an A4 letter, wedged at the bottom under a couple of exercise books. Holding it up, triumphant, she began to smooth it out, scanning the lines of typing as she did so—and groaned. "Rats. Mum's going to kill me when I tell her about this. I forgot…"

Lizzie laughed. "No she won't. Your mum's nice," she said, in a way that suggested the idea was as stupid as Amy considered Steve to be.

"Well *you* tell her then."

"Okay."

Not, for one minute, believing that her friend would actually go through with it, Amy handed over the letter and followed Lizzie to the top of the stairs. She waited there, expecting Lizzie to suddenly change her mind… but instead, her friend marched down the stairs, letter in hand, and disappeared through the door that led to the kitchen. Much to Amy's annoyance, she shut it behind her. How was she supposed to hear what they were saying now?

Sure enough, all she could make out was the faint sounds of a door-muffled conversation, followed by what was, apparently, laughter. Then the door opened again, and Lizzie made her way back up the stairs, two at a time, without the letter. She walked right past Amy, and back into the bedroom.

After a moment of stunned inaction, Amy ran along the landing and followed Lizzie through the bedroom doorway. Her friend was sitting on the window ledge again, calmly fussing with her Sindy's wedding dress. "Well?" Amy demanded. "What did she say?"

Lizzie smirked. "She said we're both dim-wits—and she'll make some chocolate buns for the stall. But don't expect anything fancy. You're getting glace icing and hundreds and thousands for the tops, because that's all she's got in."

"And she wasn't mad?"

"Not when I explained that I'd forgotten too."

"But you didn't forget!"

Lizzie fluffed out the skirt of the wedding dress. "Yes I did. I told you I didn't want to bother Mum because she was baking buns—and was mad at me for not giving her the letter about the cake stall earlier."

"You missed out that last bit," Amy grumbled.

"Yeah, I did—but I told your mum about it, and I think, knowing it's not just *her* daughter who's rubbish at remembering things, kind of helped."

"So that's what you were laughing at?" Amy asked.

Lizzie grinned. "Oh no... I told your mum that we wanted to use Steve's Action Man for our Sindys' weddings, and she said 'good luck with that', and started laughing. I just joined in with her."

"Why?"

"Not sure... because it's polite to laugh when other people do?"

Amy sighed, and shook her head in despair. "You really are a lost cause, Lizzie... but that's okay, because you got me off the hook with Mum."

To properly show her appreciation, she went over to her wardrobe and came back with a box full of ribbons—the same as she'd used for her Sindy's bouquet and headdress. "Come on, let's make something for your Sindy. Then we'll think about how to get hold of that Action Man."

For several minutes, not a lot was said. The only noise came from the rain outside, now backed by a strong wind. The window rattled.

Amy's home had once been an old coaching Inn, which meant no double-glazing and walls that were over a foot thick. The thickness of the walls meant the window ledges were more like window seats—which was nice—but the lack of double-glazing meant draughts… which wasn't so nice. Amy pulled the duvet off her bed and spread it over her and Lizzie's legs, the pair them too busy to move far.

After a while, Amy looked up and huffed out a thoughtful sigh. "What we need is a plan," she said, giving the headdress she'd made a critical once-over. "Steve always booby traps his bedroom because he thinks I might try sneaking in."

"If he didn't, you *would* sneak in," Lizzie pointed out.

"Yes… but the booby traps are really annoying. I tried getting in last week, and he'd put cotton wool all over the floor. I just thought he'd been messy, but it got stuck to my socks, and when he saw it, he told Mum—the traitor."

"It is *his* bedroom. You wouldn't like it if he came in to your room and started messing around with stuff; especially when you're not here."

Amy narrowed her eyes as she looked at her friend. "Are you sure you don't *like* my brother?"

"*Yes!* I mean, *no*… I *don't!*"

Amy kept staring for another few seconds, and then decided to let it go. "Okay. So, like I said, what we need is a plan. We need to get in to his room and get his Action Man without him knowing we've been in there. We have to be super-stealthy."

Lizzie giggled. "You make it sound like we're spies, trying to get our hands on top-secret documents."

Amy had always thought her friend had *way* too much imagination, but... "That's *exactly* what we're like; spies! We'll call this 'Operation Action Man' and if we get it right, we'll have him back in Steve's room before he even knows he's gone."

"How?" Lizzie asked.

"That depends on where my brother's put him. If he's on his bookshelf or in the toy box under his bed, that might be a problem. But if he's on top of his bed... hang on, I'll go look." Amy slipped out from the duvet and ran along the landing to Steve's bedroom door—complete with its 'No Admittance' sign. Easing the handle down, she pushed it open by a couple of inches.

"Well?" Lizzie asked when Amy got back.

"We're in luck. Action Man is on top of the bed."

"So we just go in and grab him?"

"No... I told you, Steve will have the place defended. We need something we can reach into the bedroom with from the landing. That way, I won't be breaking any rules—because *I* haven't been in his room," Amy explained.

"I don't see how that's possible," Lizzie said, frowning down at her Sindy.

"Hmm... oh, wait! I've got it!" Amy replied, almost jigging with excitement, as she dropped to all fours to peer under her bed. "Nope, not there," she muttered, before going over to her wardrobe and pulling the doors open. There was too much stuff for a clear view—but after a bit of rummaging, she came out with her prize clutched in one hand. "Yes! This is what we need!"

Lizzie's expression was worried as she stared at the length of bamboo with a pocket of green mesh at one end. "But... that's a fishing net."

"Exactly!" Amy shouted. "A fishing net we can use—to catch us an Action Man!"

"I'm not sure the Sindys will want him if he's been in a smelly fishing net," Lizzie said.

Amy laughed. "Of course they will! So long as we have a man to marry them, it doesn't matter how we got him."

Lizzie still didn't look convinced. "Are you sure about this?"

"Positive," Amy replied promptly.

"Okay... guess I'm in too then," Lizzie finally agreed.

Together, they tiptoed out of the bedroom and back along the landing. Then Amy, who was the smallest, carefully opened the door and held it open for Lizzie, who positioned herself in the centre of the gap. With one hand wrapped around the jamb and the other holding the fishing net, she leaned over, until she could reach the top of Steve's bed, and began trying to 'scoop' their prize into it.

At first, the plan was unsuccessful. The weight of the plastic toy made him difficult to lift, and they had trouble getting the edge of the net underneath. Then, when they managed *that*, they found that he had to be positioned just-right within the net, otherwise he fell straight back out onto the duvet. The minutes ticked past, and Amy noticed that Lizzie had begun to sweat. Delving into her jeans' pocket, she took out a tissue (thankfully clean) and mopped at her friend's forehead. Another attempt was made, and again the action figure began to slip back out of the net.

"*No!*" Lizzie whispered in frustration—only to stop abruptly and let out a chuckle.

"What is it?" Amy asked, trying to peek around her friend.

"His hand's got caught on the netting... he's kind of dangling underneath it, but if I'm careful..."

"Go for it!" Amy commanded.

The wedding was beautiful. The rain had stopped at last, and sunlight streamed over their make-shift ceremony. As Amy and Lizzie linked their Sindys' arms through Action Man's, they hummed the wedding march happily. The bouquets looked beautiful, and both veils stayed exactly where they should. "Do you, Sindy one, and you, Sindy two, take this Action Man to be your lawful wedded husband?" Amy intoned.

"Is that right?" Lizzie asked. "He can't marry both of them, can he?"

"Well of course he can't," Amy agreed. "He's marrying one—mine—and standing in for his twin brother with yours, because *he's* in another country at the moment."

"Oh, okay... that makes sense," Lizzie said.

"You may kiss the brides," Amy announced, moving the scarred and almost bald hero, who was still dressed in his camouflage gear, into position. "Mwah, mwah, mwah... oh my love, you are *so* beautiful, and I am such a luck..."

"*Oi! Get your mitts off my Action Man!*" an enraged voice bellowed, making both Amy and Lizzie jump.

"That was your brother!" Lizzie whispered, horrified. Her eyes frantically searched for where the voice had come from.

"I said...!"

"He's outside!" Amy squeaked, peering out the window. "He can see everything... we're going to be in *so* much trouble!"

"It was your idea," Lizzie said.

"*You* were the one who fished him off the bed!"

"Oi!" Steve bellowed again.

Amy swallowed, and decided there was only one thing for it. Opening the window, she began to lean out, readying herself to try and explain... and to this day, she had trouble believing what happened next.

One minute, Action Man was smooching a couple of Sindys, the next, he was diving into the back garden without the aid of his parachute—right into a muddy puddle. 'Oops' didn't quite cover it.

Steve never had forgiven them for that.

Boy on a Blue Bike

Cycling towards her, the boy on the blue bike wobbled, but carried on. His short brown hair was hidden under a red safety helmet, and he was as well-padded as he could be, in thick corduroy trousers and a grandma-knitted jumper. Blue eyes, bright as the bike's paintwork, and so very like his dad's, sparkled with triumph as he made his way along the quiet road, all the way from their neighbours' front door, three houses along. Shoes scraped on the tarmac as he drew closer, with not a single thought for the scuffed leather as he almost crashed into her legs—almost.

"Did you see? Did you see, Mum?!" he crowed, head tilted back, one fist punching the air in excitement.

Lizzie smiled at her son. "I did indeed, Oliver—just wait until your dad sees what you can do. He's going to be so proud of you!" She leaned down, opening her arms, ready to scoop him up into a motherly hug, but stopped herself, as awkwardly as he'd stopped his bike. "Whoops, sorry, nearly forgot!"

Oliver frowned. "I told you, Mum, I'm too big for cuddles." He paused, and then began to turn his bike, back the way he'd come. "Watch me again!" he demanded. It had been the same demand all afternoon. Lizzie was beginning to wonder if five-year-olds had renewable energy hardwired into their DNA. Just watching him made her feel tired.

"I'm watching, love," she said, and did just that, again, and again, and again… until the sound of an approaching engine had her turning to look towards the end of the road, where a large black car had just cleared the junction.

Turning back towards Oliver, she waved her arms and shouted to him, "Car coming! Get off the road!"

Feet on the floor again, Oliver manoeuvred himself and his bike to the side of the road, where Lizzie helped him up onto the pavement. She raised her hand in thanks, appreciating the fact that her friends, Norman and Maureen, who also happened to be their next-door neighbours, had waited so patiently. But when the car glided past, Oliver groaned, refusing to acknowledge the small, grinning face that was pressed up against the backseat window, and Lizzie found herself hard-pushed not to start giggling.

"Oh, no," her son whispered. "*She's* home."

Laughter under control, Lizzie sent him a small frown of reprimand. "Now don't be like that, Oliver. Ashleigh is a friend, so be nice to her. You're five already, but she's only four—remember that."

Oliver's face turned sulky. "But she's a *girl*, and she's always asking me if I want to go and play with her dolls." He opened his mouth, pulled the corners of his lips down into a grimace, and stuck his tongue out, making a kind of retching sound in the process.

"I thought she said you could take your World Wrestling figures round to her house?"

"I can't do *that*!" Oliver said, sounding horrified. "She's got Barbie dolls!"

"And?" Lizzie asked, not seeing the problem.

Oliver looked almost furtive as he glanced about him, as if expecting *Ninja* Ashleigh to sneak up on him. He beckoned Lizzie closer, only speaking when her ear was right by his mouth. "And she wants them to kiss and stuff!" He pulled back from her slightly, to show-off his ferocious glare. "Like World Wrestlers would *want* to go round kissing girls!"

He was so indignant; Lizzie had to bite the inside of her cheek to stop herself smiling. It took her a moment to get her voice pitched right, too. "Ah, yes, I see what you mean..." The smile was hovering again, but she squashed it. "I think I remember a similar thing when I was young."

"You're too old to have had a Barbie doll," Oliver pointed out.

"Yes, but I did have a Sindy, and your dad had an Action Man—same difference," she explained. Her poor son looked so puzzled by that statement; she decided to take pity on him. "All I'm saying is that your dad and I argued about this kind of stuff too, and look what happened to us."

The horror on Oliver's face intensified. "You mean... I have to marry her?"

"No!" Lizzie hung her head, trying to figure out a way to make him understand. Pulling in a breath, she aimed for a calmer response. "No, Oliver, I mean that your dad and I are best friends now, even though we used to fight when we were younger. Just because you don't like Ashleigh's Barbie dolls, doesn't mean you can't still be friends. You just have to find something you *can* play with—without getting upset with each other."

"Like what?" Oliver asked, and then frowned, jumping into speech again before Lizzie managed to get a word out. "Anyway… I bet you didn't get in the way of Dad practicing on his bike. Ashleigh keeps talking to me when I'm on mine, and then I start to wobble. It's annoying."

Lizzie refrained from mentioning that he wobbled anyway. "Actually, I do remember something about a bike, but we were quite a bit older than you are now. Your dad, and a group of his friends, once ambushed me outside my house. They were all on their bikes— and your grandma was watching the whole thing from behind the sheets she was pegging out. I was so embarrassed. I liked your dad you see, but I was a bit shy about the whole thing, and…"

"Dad did what?" Oliver asked, and then shook his head violently, the frown still in place. "Never mind, Mum—I don't think Ashleigh and me are *ever* going to get along."

Lizzie sighed, and racked her brains for something else to say. "What about Lego? You both like that don't you? You could invite Ashleigh round to play with Lego at our house, if you don't want to go round to hers."

"Hmm…" Oliver sounded as if he was actually giving the idea serious consideration. Right up until a strident voice overrode everything else.

"Oliiiiver! Oh, Oliiiiver!" a sing-song voice shouted out from somewhere behind Lizzie. Turning, she watched as Maureen emerged from their gateway, with an obviously excited Ashleigh by her side.

But not for long; Ashleigh started running as soon as she spotted Oliver, her face stretched by a huge smile, and her squeal of delight almost high enough to shatter glass.

"Yeah, Lego… no way, Mum!" Oliver shouted.

Surprised by the fact that his voice seemed to be moving away from her, Lizzie looked back at him, just as he was racing off towards his friend's house, further along the street. The sun shimmered off the blue bike, his legs were working nineteen to the dozen, and Ashleigh was in hot pursuit.

By the time Maureen charged past, intent on rescuing one of them—and Lizzie wasn't sure if she was aiming for Ashleigh or Oliver—the battle against laughter had become fiercer than ever.

So when Steve pulled up a few moments later, leaned through the car window and asked where his son was, perhaps it wasn't so surprising that Lizzie lost the war. One last, coherent thought—and she surrendered completely to a fit of giggles. *'At least he's stopped wobbling…'*

Arguing Over Victoria

It was Lily's opinion that 'The Great British Bake Off' had a lot to answer for. Before the runaway success of that particular reality show, her kitchen had been an oasis of calm, where she could mix, sieve, and beat-up innocent eggs in perfect peace—but not anymore. It seemed that anyone who was anyone had an opinion on how best to bake, and they didn't hold back when it came to telling her how she could improve her fruit pies, vol-au-vents, and everything in between.

Not that she didn't champion the whole 'home baking' movement. Hadn't she herself been baking from a young age? In fact, thinking back, she was surprised her mother hadn't gone white from the stress of it all.

She was good at baking, too. It hadn't surprised anyone when she opened-up a small tearoom called 'Cosies and Cakes' in her home village, taking advantage of the passing trade from walkers, cyclists and families on holiday, not to mention the sweet-toothed locals. As well as tea (served in a traditional teapot, covered in a brightly knitted cosy) and coffee, she offered light lunches, and a selection of cakes and pastries. She also took orders for decorated celebration cakes. It was a side of the business that had been growing steadily month by month as word spread, and more and more children wanted 'a Lily cake'.

Even now, soon-to-be-nine, Oliver Lambert, was sitting at a table with his mother. He sipped from a glass of blackcurrant cordial and tucked into a piece of chocolate cake, whilst his mother enjoyed a well-deserved cup of tea and a slice of bakewell tart. Between them lay Lily's cake book—an album filled with photos of all the cakes she'd produced so far—and they turned the pages slowly, inspecting each one with care. Given the choice, Lily preferred the challenge of one-off designs, but found that most people hadn't got a clue what could be created from sponge cake and fondant icing. Having the book for potential customers to look through often helped to kick-start their own ideas.

"I want a dragon," Oliver announced, staring at the photo of a cake where one such scaly predator was wrapped around a castle. His mother turned the page, and he frowned as he spotted a mediaeval tent, with flag flying, and a knight in a suit of armour standing beside it. "Or maybe a knight…"

Washing up in the back kitchen, but still able to see her customers, Lily ducked her head, so that no one would see the smile on her face. But a moment later, she heard Oliver's mother ask a question that had her stomach muscles tensing. "And what flavour sponge would you like? You could have chocolate, coffee, lemon, or a plain Victoria sponge with jam and cream."

A polite cough, obviously designed to attract attention, came from the direction of the table by the tearoom's window. Peeking round the kitchen doorway, Lily felt her stomach move from tense to knotted. That particular table was occupied by a group of four regular customers, all of whom liked to linger over their tea and cake. Today was no exception. Though their slices of cake were reduced to crumbs, Mrs Prescott, Mrs

Smythe, Mrs Barton and Mrs Simmons (all of them 'Bake Off' fans and members of the formidable Women's Institute) had put down their teacups, and were regarding Oliver and his mother with expressions of disapproval. Lily suppressed a groan—not one of the ladies would be afraid to offer their opinion to others; especially about baking.

Like the rest of the women at the window table, the lady who'd coughed—Mrs Simmons—was dressed in a neatly tailored tweed suit and tastefully simple sateen blouse, accessorised with highly-polished leather shoes and handbag, and discreet jewellery that had probably been handed down through the generations. Lily had often thought that if their hair styles had been rolled and pinned, it would be like looking back in time to the 1940s. Most days, thankfully, these ladies kept themselves to themselves. Today, unfortunately, when Oliver and his mother turned with regrettable, unknowing politeness towards Mrs Simmons, it was all the invitation they needed...

"A Victoria sponge should *never* be served with jam *and* cream," Mrs Simmons explained, in a tone that managed to convey that everyone and his dog should have known this.

Not surprisingly, Oliver had something to say about *that* comment. "But I like jam and cream."

Mrs Simmons looked at him without any softening of her expression, and seeing this, her companions moved in, attempting to smooth over what was fast becoming an awkward moment.

"I'm sure you do, young man," Mrs Prescott allowed, "but that's hardly the point."

Lily, about to open her mouth and intervene, bit back a laugh when Oliver's mother waded into the conversation. "Oh? And what *is* the point? I hardly think the filling in my son's birthday cake is a matter of any real importance. If he likes jam *and* cream, why shouldn't he have jam and cream?"

Mrs Barton, who looked eighty if she was a day, and who had the rather bad habit of sucking noisily on her false teeth, or popping them out during conversation, with no regard for those it might annoy or disgust, let out a gasp. "The point, my dear woman, is that a traditional, true Victoria sponge is filled with raspberry jam and nothing else. If your son wants cream as well… well, it's entirely up to you whether you spoil him and cater to his every whim, but it *won't* make his cake anything more than a plain sponge."

Oliver's mum looked flabbergasted. She turned her head to look at Lily with raised eyebrows, and an amused smile. "I had no idea that the rules on cake fillings were so strict—had you, Lily?"

But before Lily could reply, and say that she really didn't care what went in the middle of her cakes, Mrs Smythe leant forward to add her own opinion. "Children today have no concept of what is reasonable. They are excessively greedy and ask for anything and everything they think their parents will indulge them in. It's a pity that your son isn't more like my Alistair… he's never asked for anything in his life—always grateful for whatever he received."

Oliver, who was well aware of Mrs Smythe's name, even if she didn't seem to know his, stared at her with round eyes. "You called your son *Alistair*, Mrs Smythe?" he asked, sounding like he needed another gulp of cordial.

Mrs Smythe fixed him with a glare that would have done a basilisk proud. "I certainly did, young man;

Alistair is a very old family name. It means 'defender of mankind'."

Oliver, whom Lily knew was a usually polite child, snorted rudely and turned away from the now outraged women sitting by the window. "You know, I think I'll go for a Spider Man cake, Mum; if that's okay with Lily?"

Lily, who knew children well enough to realise that it was unlikely Mrs Smythe, or any of her friends, was about to be let off the hook for being so pompous, moved into the tearoom warily. Smiling at Oliver, she picked up a notepad and pencil from the pine dresser, where her beloved collection of blue and white china was displayed, and pulled up a chair next to him. "That sounds like a great idea, Oliver. Would you like a three dimensional head... I think there's a picture in the book, of one I've already done like that, or would you like something a bit different—maybe a house, with Spider Man climbing up it?"

Oliver nodded enthusiastically. "That sounds brilliant... and could you add in a villain, too?"

Lily dipped her head in agreement as she scribbled down the details. "No problem. Which one would you like—The Green Goblin or..." She glanced up at Oliver, surprised to see a wicked gleam in his eyes. Suddenly, she had a very bad feeling about what he was going to say next.

"Actually, I'd like the *Ultimate Spider Slayer*," Oliver replied. Then he paused. "You know... the evil Alistair Smythe's alter ego, a villain who won't rest until Spider Man's dead."

The saying 'you could have heard a pin drop' suddenly took on a whole new meaning for Lily. Biting her lip, she very carefully, and neatly, wrote down the words 'Alistair Smythe—Ultimate Spider Slayer' on her pad.

Was it her imagination, or was there a lot of very heavy, *angry*, breathing coming from the table by the window? Pulling in a steady breath, she risked a sideways glance at Oliver's mum. It seemed that she wasn't the only one having to bite her lip to stop laughing. "And, what flavour cake would you like?" she squeaked, praying that Oliver would show mercy and *not* go for the collective jugulars of four rather up-tight, matronly ladies.

Her prayer went unanswered.

"I'd like a Victoria sponge please; one with *lots* of lovely raspberry jam… and buttercream."

Lily was pressing down on the pad so hard, she was surprised the pencil's point didn't break, and go flying across the room.

A loud sucking noise, and the click of agitated false teeth, filled the air—Lily cringed at the inherent disapproval the sound conveyed. Chairs were scraped back loudly, and there was an indignant, harshly muttered "Well really!" before the door of the tearoom was slammed shut, leaving the bell suspended from its back tinkling wildly.

Oliver's mum sent Lily an apologetic look. "Please tell me they'd already paid," she whispered.

"Oh yes," Lily replied, glancing over at the now vacant window table. "And they left a tip too," she noted. Then she levelled her gaze on a smirking Oliver. "So… do you *really* want a Spider Man cake?"

Oliver managed to look sheepish, even as he gave a chuckle. "Yeah… but I'd rather have the Green Goblin on it, because he's a way-better villain than the Ultimate Spider Slayer—and I'd like chocolate cake, please." He pointed at the crumbs on the plate in front of him. "Because that was *awesome*—and I'm not keen on Victoria sponge."

Smiler

There she was, oblivious as usual. Oliver wasn't sure whom or what to thank for this, but the fact that he was up a ladder, with a clear view of the street, at the exact moment *she* walked by, certainly felt like providence.

He took his time admiring the view: long, gorgeous legs, shown off to perfection by a knee length, swishy-hemmed skirt; a tangle of long, mouse-brown hair, shot through with bronze strands; and curves that had always made him look twice. But the cherry on the top—as ever—was that smile. Was there any wonder he'd fallen for her?

It was just a shame that as she got closer, the inevitable happened. The smile stiffened, and then disappeared. And he only had himself to blame. Still… a chance was a chance.

"Hi there, Ashleigh," he called, in a bid to get her to slow her steps. "It's nice to see that smile of yours."

It worked, even if the expression on her face was wary. "Hello, Oliver," she replied, looking almost nervous when he began to move down the ladder towards her. Her eyes shifted downwards, until she was staring at her feet.

Having reached the pavement, he wiped his hands on his jeans, aware that fitting the house alarm had left him covered in brick dust. Glancing down at the smears of powdery red, streaked across denim, he realised that it wasn't far off the colour of Ashleigh's cheeks. He'd recently noticed that about her; that she tended to blush whenever he was nearby. At first he'd thought it was because she was still upset with him for all the aggravation he'd given her over the years, but part of him hoped it was something else... something he could use to his advantage.

Looking at her now, he cleared his throat, pulling her attention back to his face. "So, what are you up to these days; still working at the shop?" He'd taken to going in the village shop more often, after she started working there, but he hadn't seen her around for a while.

Ashleigh shook her head. "No, I've got a job at Cosies and Cakes. Lily's got so many orders for celebration cakes; she needed an extra pair of hands, to help with the café customers."

"And I bet you're perfect at it," Oliver said, nodding his head as he spoke, and remembering with pleasure all the cakes that Lily had made *him* over the years. "With a smile like yours, everyone's bound to stay for an extra coffee—especially the blokes."

When Ashleigh's mouth dropped open, he could have kicked himself. Considering his past record, she probably thought he was making fun of her. "Don't look at me like that, Ashleigh. Didn't you know that smiling is a dying art?"

She shook her head, eyebrows drawing together in disapproval. "Not really... and I think you're wrong, anyway. Lots of people smile—mine's no different to theirs."

Oliver pulled in a breath. This was it; the chance he'd been waiting for. "Rubbish," he replied, with a completely straight face. "You have the nicest smile I've ever seen, although, if I'm honest, your legs are pretty amazing, too."

He didn't expect her to laugh, and neither did she if the wide eyes, and the hand slapped over her mouth were anything to go by. For a moment or two, they just stared at each other in surprise. Then, finally, the hand was lowered, and that beautiful smile was right where it should be. "You know, Oliver, I think that's the nicest thing you've *ever* said to me."

"Which bit," he teased, "the comment about the smile, or the one about your legs?"

Ashleigh rolled her eyes in obvious exasperation, and Oliver realised it made him feel good to see her like this. She hadn't been this relaxed with him since they were next-door neighbours, which was all of ten years ago. "The smile comment, of course," she clarified.

"So…" Oliver racked his brains to come up with something, *anything*, to keep the conversation going. "Are you heading to work now or just out for a walk?"

"Just a walk—I've been holed up in the house all day. Stretching my legs seemed like a good idea."

Oliver's gaze immediately dropped, to stare at those very same legs. They *were* rather gorgeous.

But he jumped when Ashleigh took a step closer, and tapped him under the chin with her fist. "And you can cut that out. You've never shown an interest in me before, so there's no need to start pretending one now, okay?"

Oliver's mouth dropped open at that. "Who said I was never interested in you—maybe I just hid it well."

"Yeah, right," Ashleigh muttered. "So well, you treated me like I had a contagious disease."

Thinking back, Oliver supposed she had a point, and began to realise how much of an uphill struggle he had ahead of him. He did his best to look contrite, whilst quickly devising a plan of action. It was pretty obvious that, if he wanted to get anywhere with Ashleigh, he had to act *now*. This was the first time she'd really talked to him in years.

Not that he could blame her; in their teens, he'd been well aware that she had a crush on him. He'd put it down to him being the 'boy next door', and gone out of his way to put her off. *'Like an idiot,'* he thought.

Still, a full-on pursuit might be enough to get him into her good books again. He chuckled. "You know, Smiler, you're absolutely right. I behaved badly, and I think it's only right that I make up for past mistakes. How about I join you on your walk, and take you out for tea?"

The blush flooded back into Ashleigh's cheeks. She looked anywhere but directly at him; turning her gaze to first the ladder, and then his dusty clothes. "Aren't you too busy to go walking?" she asked.

Oliver shook his head. "You can't get out of it that easy, Smiler. I'm all done here, and I could do with a change of scenery. Give me ten minutes, and I'll be ready to go." He tilted his head towards the gate that led to the back of the house. "Why don't you come and wait inside? It'll give you chance to see what I've done to the place."

As temptations went, he could tell he was on to a winner. Ashleigh looked at the gate and then back at him, clearly wanting to take him up on the offer, but still unsure. Grabbing the ladder, he folded it away with a practiced move, the fingers of one hand grasping it securely, and bent to pick up his tools with the other.

"How about you get the gate? That way you'll save me a second trip."

When she went to do exactly that, he would have punched the air in triumph if he'd had a free hand. But instead, he tried not to betray a flicker of what he was feeling. She was still wary, and he needed to proceed with care.

Once through the gate, Oliver opened the door of the house and motioned Ashleigh into the kitchen. "Go right in. I won't be long; just got to stash these in the shed." He watched her expression closely as she stepped across the threshold—her curiosity easy to see.

By the time he got back to the house, Ashleigh was sitting on one of the stools by the breakfast bar, her eyes skimming over the wooden cabinets, Aga, and old Welsh dresser, complete with its display of hand-painted earthenware. Oliver hoped she liked what she saw; everything had been chosen with the age of the house in mind. Not that he could claim it was *all* down to him: his mum was a demon when it came to hunting bargains, and she'd had a great time helping her only son to furnish his first home.

"So what do you think?" he asked, surprised at how nervous he felt. To stop himself fidgeting in the ensuing silence, both hands were pushed deep into his jeans' pockets, and he rocked back on his heels, his gaze moving around the room, trying to see it through Ashleigh's eyes.

"I like it," Ashleigh replied, apparently unaware of the relief her answer caused. "It's got a lot in common with your parents' house, when you lived next door to us. Solid wood units, antique accessories, and plates that aren't just nice to look at—they look as if you could bounce them, if you know what I mean?

Everything's well made, which isn't surprising..." she trailed off awkwardly, and a quick glance showed that the blush had come back with a vengeance.

Trying to put her at her ease, Oliver nodded. "Yeah, I do know what you mean. Solid is good though. You of all people know how clumsy I can be. Remember me on a bike? It took me ages to stop wobbling all over the place, and I had more than one set of scraped knees, from falling off."

"I think trying to get away from *me* helped improve your balance," Ashleigh reminded him, her lips twisting wryly.

'Damn', Oliver silently chastised himself; he didn't want her remembering things like that. "Yeah, well, maybe my taste wasn't as good back then. Why don't you make yourself comfy in the living room?" he asked, pointing through a doorway that led onto a square hallway, and beyond that, a large seating area. "I'll run upstairs, get changed, and we can be off in a few minutes. If you fancy a drink, help yourself. There's everything you'll need in that cupboard above the kettle."

He abandoned her then, before she had a chance to start a retreat. Taking the stairs two at a time, he headed for the shower. He needed to get the brick dust off him and into some clean clothes before re-joining her downstairs.

It took him ten minutes to shower, change, and give his hair and teeth a quick brush. Feeling suitably refreshed, he walked into the living room, and was pleased to find that Ashleigh had indeed made herself comfortable. She was sitting on his sofa, legs curled under her, reading a book on antiques, which usually lived on one of the two floor-to-ceiling bookcases, set into alcoves on either side of the fireplace.

As Oliver stepped through the door, Ashleigh jolted in her seat, as if she'd been so engrossed in the book, she hadn't realised he was there. She made to uncurl her legs, her cheeks colouring again. "Sorry, I shouldn't be lounging all over your furniture like this... bad habit," she muttered—but didn't get any further than that.

Oliver had thrown himself down on the sofa next to her, arms behind his head, and legs outstretched, in what he hoped was the picture of relaxed nonchalance. He'd been kicking himself for over a decade now, and he had no intention of messing this up.

His parents had moved house when he was nineteen, about the time he realised that little Ashleigh Smith, the girl next door, had turned into a young woman whose smile was playing havoc with his libido. At the time, he thought the move was a good thing. The two of them had been on awkward 'friendly' terms all their lives, and between Ashleigh's crush and his deliberately cultivated indifference, it was a relationship that had grown progressively more strained. So for him to suddenly become attracted to her wasn't really an option. There was too much past there.

Of course, it hadn't taken him long to realise that *deciding* that something's best for you doesn't actually *make* it best for you. Ashleigh hadn't gone to University. Instead, she'd taken a cookery course at a nearby college and, when she couldn't find a job doing what she loved, had ended up working at the local shop and continuing to live with her parents. Meanwhile, Oliver had built up a thriving carpentry business, specialising in bespoke kitchens, and bought his own home. But he'd still been in the village, and Ashleigh had still been on his mind… her *and* her smile.

He tried to coax one out of her now. "I don't mind you lounging on my sofa, Ashleigh. I've already told you how much I like those legs."

It worked. Ashleigh's laugh was infectious, and it wasn't long until they were both relaxed against the sofa-back, cocooned by its softness, chuckling like old friends—like *close* friends.

"You always did say the most ridiculous stuff," Ashleigh said.

"Like what?" Oliver asked, making sure he sounded suitably affronted.

"Like when you told me that 'gullible' wasn't in the English dictionary—and I went to check! Or what about when you went with us to the seaside for the day, and I spotted those long, pointed shells in the shop on the harbour? You told me they were really unicorn horns, that had floated around in the sea, and been worn down by the waves!"

Oliver found himself laughing at the memories. "Oh, Ash, I'd forgotten about those… you really went to check about gullible?"

Ashleigh gave him a playful thump. "Yeah, I *really* did. So…" she stuck her nose in the air, "you'll have to excuse me if I don't believe you're *that* enamoured with my legs."

Oliver, still chuckling, opened his mouth to refute that idea, but she was too quick for him. She rose from the sofa, smoothing down her skirt, and turned to give him another one of those amazing smiles. "Anyway, enough of the reminiscing, are you ready for that walk yet?"

Feeling more than a little disappointed, Oliver nodded, standing up beside her. "Yeah, almost, I just have one more thing to do. If you don't mind, that is?"

"No, go right ahead," Ashleigh said, smiling up at him.

So he did.

He put his hands on either side of her face, bent his head to hers, and kissed her like he'd fantasised about doing, ever since he was nineteen. If she decided to kick him in the shins, he'd have to apologise, but heck... for now he was going to live the dream.

For one long moment, Ashleigh froze, her eyes wide open, staring into his, and her lips unresponsive—Oliver's heart began to crack. But then he felt the breath sigh out of her, watched her eyelids slowly drop, and felt her lips soften as she moved closer against him.

Pulling her to him, he wasn't sure whom or what to thank, for giving him this chance, but he thanked them anyway—because he finally had the Smiler in his arms... and the hope she'd want to stay there.

How to Kill Grass

Oliver stared at the lawn, and sighed. "It's a mess. I think it wants re-seeding. What do you think?"

His father-in-law, Norman, (Norm for short) squinted down at his work boots, scuffing one steel-capped toe over the offending vegetation. "Yeah, I reckon you're right—it's more moss than grass. Told ya that would 'appen. Grass takes work. You need to keep on top of it."

Oliver waited expectantly; but no solution was suggested. All Norm did was cock his scraggly, white-topped head to one side, stuff both his hands into his trouser pockets and continue to survey the disaster zone that was Oliver and Ashleigh's front garden.

Part of Oliver hated this. His father-in-law was an expert gardener, and only too happy to help where he could, yet here *he* was, so far from the perfect son-in-law, it was almost laughable; and all because he was the equivalent of the Grim Reaper when it came to plants. Heck, he was lucky if he could remember to water them during a dry spell.

"So... what's best for killing grass and moss?" Oliver eventually asked.

"Well—that depends," Norm replied.

Silence.

"On what?"

"On whether you do it the old-fashioned way."

This sounded promising. "Oh, yes, the old-fashioned way is definitely best," Oliver said, whilst not having a clue what that was.

"Ah... well then, you're goin' t' need a yard brush." Norm said, nodding as he spoke.

A what? "Why would I need one of those?"

Norm pursed his lips, as if trying to find the right words; words simple enough for Oliver to understand, that is. "To brush the grass with," he said, eventually. "In the mornin' you brush it towards the sunrise, an' in the evenin' you brush it towards the sunset. Do that, for five days in a row, an' yer grass'll die off in no time."

That sounded... bizarre. But what did Oliver know? Still, he'd better check he'd heard him correctly. No sense in brushing the grass if he didn't need to.

Norm assured him, gravely, that he had it exactly right. "Make sure the brush has stiff bristles, mind... nowt flimsy!" he warned.

Oliver considered asking his wife what she thought... after all, Ashleigh was well aware that her Dad liked to play practical jokes. What if this was one of them? He gave Norm a hard stare. There wasn't even a glimmer of a smile; he seemed serious enough. Would she know if this was a wind-up? Then again, if he asked her about it, she might think he was trying to weasel his way out of the job... and he knew he'd never hear the end of *that*.

So instead, much to his neighbours' amusement, Oliver did as he'd been told, and brushed the lawn, from one end to the other, twice a day.

Despite burning cheeks, he figured it would be worth it. The doubters would be laughing on the other side of their faces soon enough.

Two days later, the grass started to turn brown. Delighted, Oliver began to brush it with renewed vigour. By the fifth day, it was definitely on its last legs.

"Do I need to keep brushing it?" he asked, when his father-in-law came to watch him on the final evening.

"No need to overdo it," Norm replied.

Finished at last, Oliver leaned on the yard brush and surveyed his handiwork with pride. The lawn was definitely dying. "Wow. You know, I'm ashamed to admit this, but I did wonder if you were having me on... but it really worked."

"Seems so," Norm agreed. "Course—it could also be that weed killer I put on last week… when Ashleigh told me you wanted to re-seed. Never could beat a bit of Glyphosate for jobs like this."

If Tinsel Babies Ruled the World

Four-year-old Laura bounced up and down as her mother, Ashleigh, tried to position tinsel on her costume *without* sticking a pin in her over-enthusiastic daughter.

"Please stay still, Ra-ra, I don't want to slip with one of these," Ashleigh pleaded, realising yet again how appropriate the nick-name was. Laura's brother, James, had christened her with it. Even now, suspended in the doorway beside them and watching his sister with obvious adoration, he mimicked her constant up-and-down motion by kicking sturdy legs against the floor, until his baby-bouncer sent him jumping into the air. His delighted crow of "Ra-ra, Ra-ra," delivered at the top of youthful lungs, was a familiar daytime soundtrack. Give the pair of them pom-poms, and they'd pass for cheerleaders.

Laura bounced again, giggling when James immediately copied. Taken by surprise, Ashleigh withdrew her hand, the pin she'd been about to carefully ease through fabric jabbing her in the hand instead. She sucked in a sharp breath, an even mix of pain and maternal relief. Trying to position the tinsel like this had been a bad idea. She'd just have to do it on the flat, and guess where it would look best.

"Ooh… *poor* Mummy," Laura suddenly cried, picking up her mother's hand so that she could inspect the bright bead of blood that welled from the pin-prick. "If Tinsel Babies ruled the world—no one would ever get hurt. Shall I kiss it better for you?"

Ashleigh smiled at her daughter, but gently pulled her hand away. Blood on the white shift-dress would be a *very* bad idea. "No, love, don't worry, I'll put a plaster on it as soon as we get this dress off you." She fished a tissue out of her pocket, wrapping it around her hand before starting to gently ease Laura out of the simply sewn, white lining material—with only a couple of pieces of tinsel in place. Arms obediently in the air, Laura still wriggled as Ashleigh pulled the dress up over her body. A pin snagged on her hair, just as Laura's head had completely disappeared into the costume, and the operation stalled. Giggles ensued, and more wriggling, until the obstruction had been carefully freed, and Laura with it.

Transferring the outfit to the dining table, Ashleigh told her two rambunctious offspring to behave as she headed for the First Aid kit in the kitchen. She could still see them both through the doorway, but had to take her eyes off them for a few brief seconds as she rummaged for a plaster and began to apply it.

That was when the crash sounded.

With plaster on crooked, Ashleigh ran back into the dining room, her head filled with thoughts of child-endangering catastrophes. Her eyes found James who, for once, was motionless in his bouncer, with eyes wide and rosebud lips silently parted. Saliva ran down his chin, glistening in the overhead light. But other than the dribble that had soaked into his top, he seemed fine. She turned her attention to the rest of the room. Laura was standing in the middle of the dining table, her costume held up in front of her, and poised like a ballerina in tights and vest. With her soft blonde curls, she would have looked angelic, if it wasn't for the shocked contrition in her huge blue eyes. Ashleigh narrowed her own in confusion. Laura looked fine too… her gaze rested on the chaos of the floor. 'Fine' could not, apparently, be said of Ashleigh's sewing box.

Whatever Laura had been doing, it had resulted in the sewing box sliding from the table-top, its contents scattered across the carpet.

"What on earth…" Ashleigh began, only to be interrupted by Laura's childish, tearful voice.

"If Tinsel Babies ruled the world—no one would get mad, Mummy."

Ashleigh wanted to be angry, but… she rubbed her hand across the slight swell of her stomach, the action almost a habit these days. Oliver would say it wasn't good for her—or the baby. Sighing, she raised her eyes to those of her daughter… and something inside melted. "It's okay, Ra-ra. Be a good girl, and stay on the table until I've cleared everything up again. There are pins and needles everywhere…"

Laura nodded, her expression still tearful, and promptly sat down, cross-legged, on top of the dining table. Making sure that every sharp, metallic sewing aid was replaced in the box, along with hooks-and-eyes, press-studs, buttons, spools of cotton, and lengths of elastic and emergency wonder-web, Ashleigh was all too aware of her daughter's watchful gaze. But only when she was completely satisfied that the carpet was a safe place for her children to play, did she look up again. Laura's eyes were huge and solemn. "If Tinsel Babies ruled the world—accidents wouldn't happen," she whispered.

In the background, James began to make loud, expertly delivered raspberry-sounds. Glancing at him, Ashleigh saw that a copious amount of teething-dribble was accompanied by bubbles, cascading from his grinning mouth. Smiling back at him, she turned towards Laura, standing as she did so, and set the sewing box back on the table. Then she scooped her daughter up onto one hip and carried her over to James.

"Mumm-um-um… Ra-ra-ra," James said.

"I need to get him out of his bouncer," Ashleigh told Laura. With both of them kneeling, she quickly unfastened the baby-bouncer straps and lifted her cheerful, raspberry-blowing son into her arms.

"What's that smell?" Laura asked, wrinkling her nose.

Ashleigh groaned. "Oh no…"

"If Tinsel Babies ruled the world—poo wouldn't smell that bad," Laura announced.

Ashleigh couldn't help laughing at that. "Come on, you can sit and keep me company whilst I get this little tyke sorted. I'm thinking clean bottom, warm milk, a bath, and bed. If Daddy's back in time, he can read you both a bedtime story, whilst I get on with your costume. What do you think to that idea?"

"Can I get in the bath with him?" Laura asked.

"Yes."

"Then… I like that idea, Mummy."

It was 11pm when Oliver poked his head around the dining room door and frowned at his wife. "You're *still* at it?"

Ashleigh smiled at him around the two pins she had clamped between her teeth, and nodded. Reaching up, she took hold of the pins, and deftly fixed the last of the tinsel in place. "Not long now. A few more stitches and it's ready to go. Are the kids still asleep? James's teeth have been annoying him today…"

Oliver walked over to her. "They're both sound asleep, thank goodness." He ran a hand over the white and silver costume. "You've made a good job of this. Laura's going to be thrilled when she sees it finished— she's so excited about tomorrow. I thought she was going to bounce right out of bed earlier. I read them both three stories, and though James went out like the proverbial light, it took our secret weapon to get Laura's eyes drooping."

Picking up a needle and thread, Ashleigh laughed as she started to slide it in and out of the fabric. "Let me guess… Dr Seuss's Sleep Book?"

Oliver nodded, his return chuckle sounding tired. "Yeah—works every time." He paused, before moving behind her to press his hands to the muscles of her neck. Still stitching, she leant back into the rolling action of his palms and fingers. The firm, circling motion of his thumbs eased the knots of tension from her shoulders. Bending down to drop a kiss below her ear, he whispered the question she'd hoped for. "Do you want a coffee?"

"Oh, yes… but not coffee. If I have that now, I definitely won't get any sleep tonight. Make it a hot chocolate and I'll love you forever."

With his lips still pressed against her neck, Oliver chuckled, the sound vibrating against her skin. Closing her eyes on a sigh, Ashleigh stopped sewing, and hoped he knew that it was moments like this that made life worthwhile. She was almost sorry when he gave her shoulders one last squeeze and straightened up—but the thought of a hot drink warred with her need for a neck massage.

"I thought you were already going to love me forever, but I'll get you that chocolate anyway. You deserve it after the day you've had." He paused in the kitchen doorway, sending her an amused look. "Of course, if Laura was here right now, I have a pretty good idea what she'd be saying..."

Ashleigh smiled, adding more stitches to her daughter's costume. "If Tinsel Babies ruled the world— hot chocolate would be on tap."

The village hall was filled to capacity, with every chair taken by proud friends and relatives. Ashleigh knew that most people wouldn't understand the amount of work that had gone into this performance—a one-night-only event—or *why* she, along with other Mums, Dads and Grandparents had bothered. But it was more than an amateur play; it was the coming together of the youngest members of their families, all of whom wanted to raise money for charity in a way that relied on the talents of a large proportion of the village's residents. A teenager, who'd babysat for some of the children in the play, had written the story it was based on. She'd taken inspiration from the toys those children loved, and found a way to include all who wanted to participate... right down to those who were Laura's age.

The hall had been a part of village life since the 1940s, bringing people together for dances, clubs, coffee mornings, and amateur dramatic events like this one. As the stage curtain rose, and clear, eager, childish voices repeated the lines they'd practiced for weeks, Ashleigh wondered if the people who'd built the hall would have enjoyed this latest venture.

The first half of the production went off with barely a hitch, followed by an interval that lasted well over half an hour. Cakes and cups of tea, packets of crisps and fruit cordial were served for a nominal fee, swelling the charity coffers a little more, and encouraging people to chat over their refreshments. It wasn't long before the break in proceedings took on a party atmosphere. Then it was time for the audience to return to their seats, and the curtain rose once more... In the final scenes, the narrator warned the evil 'Raven' that he could never win against the forces of goodness, especially when the smallest, most powerful fairies in the playroom—the Tinsel Babies—were waiting in the wings.

Lights dimmed, and the bouncy, cheerful notes of the *Popcorn* song crackled from the sound-system, heralding the opening of two doors, one on either side of the stage. Out from these flowed lines of happily skipping and dancing children, all dressed in white, with glinting, silver tinsel curled around dresses and leotards. They circled the hall and audience, holding tight to ropes of yet more tinsel, before snaking their way along the central aisle and up onto the stage. Under the carefully positioned spotlights, it was as if a river of silver and smiles had invaded the crowded space—and it didn't take long for the 'bad guys' to be overwhelmed by a glittering mass of 'goodness'.

In amongst it all, with her eyes shining and a smile that looked as if it might split her face in two, was Laura—who couldn't resist a wave at her parents and brother.

James, who'd been incredibly good, sitting *mostly* quiet on his mum's knee or dozing on his dad's shoulder, was wide awake now. He raised his chubby arms in salute to his sister, the saliva dribbling from his mouth unabated, as he shouted with delight. "Ra-ra, Ra-ra, Ra-ra!"

Looking round at the teary eyes of the audience and the pride that set the children's faces aglow, Ashleigh felt her throat begin to tighten. The happy tears that she'd been trying to swallow escaped, sliding down her cheeks, even as she clapped until her hands were sore.

Openly laughing at her, Oliver leaned across and wrapped an arm around her, whilst still keeping a tight hold on James. His shouted words reached her over the applause. "So it's official: If Tinsel Babies ruled the world—the world would be a better place."

Ashleigh couldn't agree more.

Bonfire Night

I love bonfire night.

As a child, every family seemed to celebrate the foiled Gunpowder Plot. It was a good excuse to get rid of the garden rubbish, and there was a sense of excited anticipation as night time fell; bringing with it the smell of wood-smoke, and the delighted shrieks of children up and down our street. We'd dine on old favourites: baked potatoes with butter, cups of tomato soup, a hotdog with fried onions. Flavours and textures I can still recall. Soft and fluffy, with earthy overtones, salt and cream; thick liquid, so hot it burned my tongue with its smooth, tangy richness; layers of meat and fat, with a hint of slow-cooked caramel, overlaid with the bright, peppery sharpness of mustard, and sweetly-sour ketchup.

Then we'd move outside, in orderly, wool-wrapped procession, ready to ooh and ah at twinkling fountains and rockets that raced skywards with a soft *phfft*. I liked the rockets, but my brother, James, lived for the bangers and screechers, and my sister, Jane, always stared, wide-eyed, at the sparkler in her hand. No one really liked the Catherine Wheels; they never worked properly.

Mum hated the lot of them.

After years of family bonfires, the voice of reason began to intrude. Wouldn't this all be better if we worked together? Larger displays became the norm, with everyone taking their fireworks to a single venue, pooling fire-fuel and refreshments. The anticipated show of light and chemistry-driven colour was extended; sometimes for hours.

But that didn't last long. So many people, all bringing boxes of tiny fireworks that were all the same and took ages to light... surely there was a better way?

Entry fees were the answer, of course. No need to worry about a thing. Just give us the money you *would* have spent, and we'll organise everything... maybe we could hire somewhere? More people could come then.

Only it didn't work.

The bigger the crowds, the bigger the fireworks they demanded; the bigger the fireworks, the more dangerous the job of letting them off; the more dangerous the job, the more qualified you needed to be; the more qualified you needed to be... and only the professionals would do.

Money, money, money, and suddenly, bonfire night was for fundraising; a sure thing, taken over by charities and business. Entry charges for children and adults alike—higher if you want to bring your car. There were charges for food, for the light-up toys that every child *has* to have, lest bonfire night be ruined... and charges for entertainment whilst you wait for the display to start. Everyone's a winner!

It spirals on, round and around, better than any Catherine Wheel. But the bigger the display, and the more money made, the fiercer the competition. A single night is never enough. Some years it's almost a week of fireworks, with commerce firmly in charge.

I remember the moment my pleasure shattered. I was standing in a muddy field, surrounded by strangers, and feeling lost. There was pushing and shoving in the queues for food, the same by the ropes that cordoned off the display area, and at the end of the night, impatient drivers would be jostling for pole position and the quickest way home.

Where had the joy of *my* bonfire nights gone?

It had imploded, leaving me to mourn the loss of those simple, back-garden events—until a phone call from my sister brought hope sneaking back.

Time-travel is a state of mind.

Now we pool our resources and talents. Jane whips up delicious homemade food, James acts as fire marshal, and I make sure that everyone has a drink. Then we stand around the bonfire, our faces aglow, and watch in wonder. *Our* children ooh and ah as colours burst across the sky, and they giggle at the fizz, crackle and hiss of bright stars and sparks. Nothing much has changed. The fireworks have got better, and are definitely bigger, and Mum still hates the lot of them.

There are still those who like the rockets best, others who enjoy the frenetic noise, and some who only want to draw patterns in the air, with their arms outstretched and sparklers grasped tight. Catherine Wheels *still* don't work.

I *love* bonfire night.

Old China

The china cabinet had come from Lily's house, and before that, it had held pride-of-place in the café she'd run. Polished mahogany, inlaid with bands of paler wood, balanced above elegant, tapering legs. Graceful, curved glazing bars held sections of old, rippled glass in place. Inside, there was an array of china that most people would overlook, simply because they considered it too old fashioned. When she thought about it, Jane was amazed that it had survived its time in a public area, where children had regularly run about the place.

But Jane loved it. Lily had been her Godmother, and as far as she was concerned, there wasn't a better woman her parents could have chosen. Her eyes stung as she looked at the cabinet, the grief of Lily's death still too fresh; she'd lost a Godmother, a friend, a one-time employer, a wise counsel. The hole that had been left in Jane's life was difficult to describe to anyone who hadn't suffered a similar loss. And anyway, part of her didn't want to describe it. It was too private.

Lily had been a close friend of Jane's parents, Ashleigh and Oliver, too. Her dad would go on about the wonderful birthday cakes she'd made for him when he was younger. Rich chocolate confections, covered in fondant icing, and crafted into shapes that had never failed to widen his eyes with delight: Dragons, castles, knights and heroes. Her mum had helped out in Lily's café, long before Jane or her elder brother and sister had come on the scene. Their entire family had loved Lily.

So when Jane learned that Lily had left her the china cabinet, she'd clung to her mum and cried out her heart—and her mum had understood. The cabinet was a part of Lily; filled with the delicate china she'd only used on special occasions, with gifts that grateful customers had brought back from their travels abroad, and with ornamental figures that had belonged to Lily's mother and grandmother. Jane knew the histories of each and every piece, had listened with fascination as her Godmother told her the stories behind the prettily patterned and expertly modelled treasures.

Today they had found a new home, in Jane's living room. She'd been careful about its positioning, and Mum had helped her. They'd made sure that there was a light nearby, that would illuminate them day or night. She was sitting in that room now. Mum had gone home, and Jane had poured herself a sherry-glass of Lily's favourite liqueur. It felt right to raise it to her Godmother's memory, as she admired the items that Lily had loved so much.

"To Lily," Jane whispered. "I hope you know how carefully I'll guard the items and memories within your cabinet. I won't forget their stories, just as I won't forget you."

The glass tipped back, and a sip was taken, the tangy, fruit laden scent like a memory in itself; of Autumnal bounty. The rich flavours, of apple and bramble, teased their way along her taste buds, the thickly-sweet liqueur sliding down her throat; warm, and soothing. Yet, for all its richness, it was a strangely bright drink, too. A little old fashioned, perhaps, just as

Lily and her china cabinet had been, but still, none of that dimmed the pleasure it gave.

Thinking about her Godmother now, Jane was shocked to realise that she'd never asked Lily about her life; why she was on her own, unmarried. The rational part of her knew that this was because Lily had never seemed forlorn, not for a single moment, but the more emotional part of her felt as if she should have made the effort—should at least have asked.

Lily had given the impression that she was a woman who'd done everything she'd ever wanted to, and was content with her life: tending a café in a small village. She'd loved to bring a smile to the face of others, through her talent for creating delicious food, and she also seemed to enjoy giving them a place where they could gather with their friends, shelter from the weather or simply indulge a sweet tooth. They'd drawn her into their lives through the conversations they'd shared with her, over cups of tea and sweet treats. But where had the love, happiness, adventure and culture been in Lily's life? Had she wanted any of those—had she experienced them earlier in her life?

Jane frowned, staring hard at the cabinet. Had Lily minded that nobody asked about *her*, being too focused on their own lives, or had that been her intention—to hide in plain sight?

It was as though the cabinet called to her. She found herself getting up from her chair and going to stand in front of it. There was a tiny, iron key, with a crown-shaped bow, sitting in the keyhole. And with suddenly shaking fingers, Jane reached out and turned it, feeling the slight resistance of the lock, before it clicked open, and the glazed door swung outwards; a smooth motion on well-oiled hinges.

"It's like opening the door to her life, to everything she valued," Jane murmured. Not that she meant the china itself—but the memories each piece embodied.

Her gaze skimmed across hand painted Coalport, the fine porcelain enamelled in jewel-bright colours, with sweeping borders around central plaques. The aptly named 'cabinet plates' were decorated with images of birds, flowers and fruit, the pallet so fresh and vibrant, she could almost believe they had been painted yesterday. But it wasn't a plate that caught her eye—it was a box. Jane remembered how her mother, who'd helped her to transfer the treasures, had paused when handling it. Curious, she leaned forward, picking it up from its place on the centre shelf.

The main colour was a rich turquoise, edged with the same liberal gilding as the Coalport, but there was something different about the painting. On the lid, a posy of simple blue flowers, with yellow centres, nestled amidst lush, green leaves. "Forget-me-nots," Jane said out loud, smiling as she ran a gentle finger across them. Then she opened it, delighted to find that there were more forget-me-not blooms painted on the lid's underside. There was a piece of paper too, folded several times, until it fitted the small space. Jane couldn't remember having seen the box before, which was odd, as Lily had often opened the cabinet for her. She hated to think it, but maybe she'd forgotten? Plucking the paper from inside, she hoped it would give her some idea of where the box had come from, and how it came into Lily's possession.

It did... but not in the way that Jane had expected, giving a brief resume of dates, factory and place of purchase. The paper was actually a letter—addressed to her.

To my dear Jane,

I know, when you read this, I will be dead, and that my solicitor will have done as I requested, and placed this box in the china cabinet. I have always intended for to you to have the cabinet—because you, more than anyone else, recognised the true value of the objects on display.

I enjoyed telling you the stories behind how each item came to me, but this box—this box is the only object I found I couldn't share. Not even with you, my dear.

It is something that I have kept, for my eyes only, for a very long time; and for a while I even thought that I would take it to my grave. But it's far too lovely for that, and I know that you will appreciate its beauty, and keep it safe, just as you will care for my other treasures.

The box is French, by a company called 'Bourdois & Bloch' and made (I believe) in the late 19th Century. But I did not receive it, as a gift, until 1958. It came from my own Godmother, with a tale of such sadness; I could never have put it on display.

You see… my Godmother was a close friend of my mother's. Or rather, as I later discovered, my Godmother was actually my mother, and my mother was my adoptive mother. Not that it shows on any official register. It was something that happened in a time when these things were simply done that way… women were sent into 'confinement' and babies were handed over to other couples and passed off as their own flesh and blood. That is what happened to me, and I could never blame them for it. I had a wonderful childhood, and wonderful parents, and my birth mother was unable to care for me as she should. It's the war I blame, and the horrors it forced on innocent people.

But they kept in touch, and they made sure I grew up knowing her as someone loving in my life.

My birth mother, Eileen Cade, was a British operative, dropped over enemy lines in France, and my father, coincidentally, was a boulanger—an ordinary working man, who was also part of the resistance movement. That's how my parents met... and he is the one who gave her the box, which she later passed to me.

I won't dwell on the details of their affair, or on the sadness of its outcome, but I did want you to realise that this box is, and always has been, my most treasured possession. It's also the reason that I felt a need to honour my roots, by using the talent I had so obviously inherited. That is why I opened the café and started the celebration cake side of the business— because for me, every day in that tiny kitchen was a celebration of everything my parents had given me. The freedom to live my life the way I wanted, and to make friends with ordinary people; who, when you look closely, rarely are ordinary.

I have loved the life that my family gave me, both biological and adoptive, and I was honoured to call you my Goddaughter, Jane.

Please, do not grieve for me too long—live your life and enjoy your family and friends. They need your compassion and care far more than I.

With much love, and Best Wishes for your future,
Lily xxx

The tears were running down Jane's face by the time the last word was read, and it took her a long time to refold the letter, to place it back in the box, and put the box on the shelf with a steady hand. It took even longer to close the cabinet door; the key stiff in the lock.

But Lily was right. There were worse things than death. There was living a life unconnected to others, without the knowledge that love and sacrifice are everywhere—and should be honoured. Love could take many forms, as Lily's parents (all of them) had shown. And a fulfilled life wasn't always about adventure and excitement, because sometimes the most satisfying experiences are right in front of you, every day.

Sitting back on her chair, with thoughtful gaze still trained on the cabinet, Jane gave silent thanks for the wonderful woman her Godmother had been. Then she glanced at the living room clock. It was only 9pm. There was still time to give Mum a ring... and thank her for her help: today and always.

Love Came Down At Christmas

The church, predictably, was packed. Faces were tilted upwards, turning this way and that, eyes wide as they took in the atmosphere that only seemed to exist at this time of year, and in *this* service. The Christingle service... a celebration of light.

Everything had taken on a dream-like feel. The life-sized nativity, lit in such a way that children of all ages could almost believe it was real; the stone pillars wreathed with thick greenery and tall candles, interspersed by the subtle glow of red berries; the tree, shining under a layer of tinsel and glass baubles (the yearly donation of a local farmer and his family); the advent banner.

It turned a cold building, of stone and stained glass, into something more.

Perhaps a glimpse of another world? Ashleigh wondered.

Staring across the church's void, she was pleased with her vantage point, easily able to pick out the faces of those who always joined her here—it was, after all a tradition. Golden faces, filled with the warmth and beauty of a candle flame.

Mr Carr, Uncle Rob, Lily, Mum and Dad, the grandparents... they look younger. Maybe it's true? Candlelight becomes everyone...

The thoughts ran through Ashleigh's mind, with the speed of excitement behind them, and as the service progressed, she sang the carols with gusto, her voice not as strong as it once was, lower than the other ladies' sopranos, and probably slightly off key. Truth be told, with that many voices, hers became lost amongst them. Not that it mattered. This was what Christmas was all about. Everyone together: strangers, church regulars, friends and family... with the memories of past years, and past connections, filling in the cracks—that a shining face sometimes tried to hide.

Ashleigh's eye rested on Oliver—still so handsome, despite the greying hair and life-softened skin, where brown age-spots and a map's worth of fine lines had taken up residence. She loved to see him in his long, dark, woollen coat, his posture regiment-straight, though his height had diminished. And she loved how he still insisted on wearing that old, bobbly scarf, neatly tucked around his neck. *She'd* made him that... and he'd always said it was the time she'd taken over it that meant so much to him. Heck, who was she trying to kid? She simply loved *him*.

Directly beside him, with her hand in his, stood Laura; their eldest daughter, with James and Jane beside her. Their husbands and wife, their children, and grandchildren, filled two whole pews, and Ashleigh beamed with pleasure at the sight of them.

The time came for the children to line the aisle, Ashleigh and Oliver's great-grandchildren joining in. Small fingers, wrapped around an orange that was decorated with a white candle, red ribbon, and fruits and nuts. Youthful faces took on a look of concentration. A hush of expectation rippled across the congregation.

Then came the moment when every electric light was doused, leaving only the glow of the candles, and the sound of the children singing... the moment Ashleigh had been waiting for; when she felt the urge to cry from the simple beauty of it, and fought to retain a semblance of dignity.

"Candlelight, burning bright, chase the darkness of the night...

There's a world I'm dreaming of, where there's peace and joy and love..."

The words had changed over the years, a new song for a new generation, but the innocence and hope in the faces all around her were the same. Ashleigh began to count, her eyes meeting those of her loved ones as she waited. One, two, three—the unaccompanied children continued with the song, nearing the last bar of music— four, five, six... and silence fell. A pause in time itself as the voices died away and the congregation took breath.

"Ashleigh..." Oliver murmured, his elderly face transformed by a look of wonder, as he stared straight at her. He always did remember to show her how much he cared.

Ashleigh let the tears go at last. *"Merry Christmas, my love,"* she replied, grateful for the deep connection they'd shared for so long, and always would.

But the service was over, the doors of the church opening wide as the congregation began to leave, the candles guttering in the draught from outside. Fading to nothing more than the scent of smoke... even those that were high on the pillars, where Ashleigh and her loved ones gazed out at the people they'd come to visit—even if all they could manage was a memory, held deep within a candle flame.

For what is Christmas without love? Love from the past, love in the present, and the hope of more for the future.

Chances And
Happy Endings

Like Winter Sunshine

Amy enjoyed walking. Since she was old enough to roam the countryside without adult supervision, her legs had carried her to where she needed to be—to where solitude allowed her to dream.

She felt sorry for today's children. The time when they could look to the horizon, and use their independence to explore the world around them, seemed to come later and later with each passing year. Little wonder, with all the terrible news stories that were paraded in front of worried, protective parents; some days it seemed as if every woodland, every farm building, and every quiet country lane, *must* conceal a serial killer or predatory paedophile. And even if they didn't... was it really worth the risk?

In Amy's experience, solitary walkers were viewed with suspicion too. She'd lost count of the number of cars that had slowed as they passed her, their occupants peering out the windows with lowered brows and open-mouthed surprise. She could almost hear their thoughts: *Where was her reason for being out there, alone? Where was her dog, her children or walking-group? Why would anyone go walking on their own—unless they were up to no good, or mentally challenged?*

Amy was neither. She told herself that she went walking for exercise, nothing more and nothing less, though this was, apparently, not the 'done thing' for a single woman. Jogging would have been a more acceptable pastime (so she could out-run those serial killers?), or paying through the nose to join a health club, where she could work-out on cycles (not real bikes), treadmills (not real roads), rowing machines (not real boats) or lift weights (*real* torture). But then, why would she want to do any of that, when she could pull on a pair of walking shoes and head out to the countryside around her home—for free?

Especially on a day like today; one of those mysterious, winter days, that enticed her to open her front door, and walk her way to warmth. Who could ignore such a call? She stepped out briskly, into a mist-softened morning, dressed in jeans and boots, a baggy jumper, thickly padded coat, and knitted scarf and gloves. A wide woollen band secured her hair, its colour echoing the rich-brown tones of the fly-away strands. It protected her ears and the top of her head from the cold, but the bulk of her long hair hung free, to dance behind her like an unruly pennant.

Once the last of the village's houses were behind her, the fields opened out on either side, stretching out to the Yorkshire Wolds on one side, and the river Humber on the other. In the background she could hear the constant buzz of rubber on tarmac, announcing the exodus of those heading for larger towns—and work-day routine. Cars passed her with nonchalant speed, their nearness to the narrow footpath buffeting her with waves of displaced air. Until gradually, the sound of her footsteps, brisk and even, grew evermore dominant, announcing the arrival of post rush-hour peace, where only the voice of the wind and the warble of birdsong competed.

She noted how the early-morning mist was slow to clear today. It obscured the landscape behind drifts of low-lying cloud, blocking out all but the staunchest of sunbeams. Not that Amy minded. In this dimly-lit world, she was free to build her fantasies, her thoughts flitting from potential dangers lurking in the shadows, to romantic heroes striding out from a dramatic, swirling background, to the strange, dark outlines of the trees along her route. The latter looked like upwards-reaching roots—as if the Earth, plundered of its riches, desperately sought sustenance from the air…

The idea made her frown, then smile at the whimsy of it and, not for the first time, she realised that she found the fog restful. It took away the need for concentration, obscuring the scenery like a curtain of gauze. Colours were dulled; a host of muted greens and blues, with only the occasional splash of hazy gold, held within the petals of verge-side aconites, or the brick-red hues of nearby roof-tops to enliven the scenery.

She turned right, walking towards the hamlet of Everthorpe. The road became single-track, with wide swathes of grass on either side, backed by tall hedges. In places, these hawthorn barriers, thick with sharp defences, had been ruthlessly cut through, to form simple gateways. Damp ground, scarred by heavy machinery, bore witness to the importance of agriculture in this part of Yorkshire. Wide-tracked wheels had churned the earth into a mass of chaotic ridges, with puddles of rainwater lining the deepest ruts. In the distance, Amy heard the throaty, rock-star roar of a tractor engine, the direction of the sound distorted by the fog. *'In the field or farm yard?'* she wondered, stopping to listen. But it was impossible to tell, just as it was impossible to know whether it was *him* driving the machine. If it was... there'd be no steady gaze following her today, no chance meeting and ready smile. Disappointment twisted her stomach, followed by a sharp, mental reprimand. Life had leached too much joy from her soul already. It was a lesson she needed to remember.

With a shake of her head, she set off once more, traversing the roadway with clockwork precision, her steps taking on the beat of ticking seconds.

The boundary of Everthorpe was marked by a handsome nameplate, carved from a mill-wheel and set into a framework of local stone. Amy had always liked it. It had character, and suited the tiny community, where farming had been the main source of employment for hundreds of years.

Walking on, she saw that the fog still lingered in the hamlet; softening the sharp-edged façades of each dwelling, until they appeared to be the perfect embodiment of what rural homes could and should be. Truth be told, Amy didn't think there was enough of that kind of thing. Harsh reality had become the order of the day, with dreams and romantic idylls abandoned, mocked, or ignored. That was why she mourned the loss of innocent, childish freedom; although maybe she'd change her mind on that, if she ever had children of her own?

She suspected, like the mist surrounding her, that the real world was a complex mix of light and dark— but was it right to stick to the clear brightness of days filled with winter sunshine, when the twilight world she witnessed now was so beautiful? She couldn't help laughing out loud at the thought. Her walk, as ever, had turned her into a philosopher.

"And what makes you laugh, on a morning like this, lass?"

The voice shocked Amy. Wrapped in her thoughts, her gaze had dropped to the road, leaving her unaware of anything else.

Looking up, she saw that she had almost reached Everthorpe's opposite boundary, where the sky was finally visible; the strengthening sunlight fighting back, to reveal a wash of blue.

In her peripheral vision, a man she recognised all too well was leaning over a wooden, five-bar gate. Roughly dressed, with a stubble-darkened jawline, and hair askew, he definitely looked dangerous enough to be a serial killer... one whose jackdaw eyes laughed at her without mercy. Equally, he could be, and was, the man who'd tormented Amy for too many years. They'd known each other since childhood, and she was of the opinion that three decades of hard labour should have aged his good-looks into work-worn insignificance. But life never was fair, and seeing him was something of a treat—even when he deliberately set out to irritate her.

"Wouldn't you like to know, Toby Jewitt?" she replied.

The man's smile had transferred itself from his eyes to his lips. "Haven't I just said so, Miss Amy? Or 'as the fog blocked your ears an' swaddled your brain?"

"Not so I'd noticed, and I thought we'd agreed that you'd stop calling me 'Miss' Amy? I'm not a spinster school marm, you know."

Thick, dark brows climbed... and stayed there, suspended over bright, intelligent eyes, with wickedness in their depths. "You tellin' me I'm wrong?" Toby asked, his accent thickening. "That you don't tutor English, an' are married now?"

The flush that stole across Amy's cheeks held the sting of past betrayal. Toby Jewitt was cruel indeed… to breathe life into memories she'd believed long-dead. Tears crowded at the backs of her eyes, blurring the countryside far more than any fog.

But she didn't answer, choosing to continue her walk instead. The details of a love rejected were her business alone—and Toby Jewitt could go whistle if he thought any different.

There was a muttered curse, the rattle and creak of a quickly vaulted gate, the shadow of her tormentor by her side, and a hand that caught her arm and pulled her to a stop.

Like the devil himself, his touch burned her where it rested. "I'm still here, Amy."

And how did she answer that? "I don't understand what you mean."

"Oh, I think you do. Haven't I been patient long enough? Haven't I waited for the wounds to heal, and watched over you for more years than I care to count? But I've seen those looks… the longing that matches mine whenever we meet. Out here, nature rules everything in sight, and only the people who recognise that matter. People like us." Shock held her motionless, allowing him to stroke a work-toughened finger down her cheek. It was a gesture of surprising gentleness, from a man she'd thought anything but. "And, God knows, I've made those meetings happen as often as I could. If not for those looks, I'd have given up long ago… but they gave me hope. Hope that had me keep on at ya, teasing ya till your eyes spit fire at me, and I knew my lass was almost ready; to take a chance on another man."

"But… you never said. All this time, I've been roaming these lanes like a lost soul, trying to make sense of the world and my place in it. *Why* didn't you say anything?"

The touch of his finger became an entire hand—cradling her head. Then his free arm curled around her, pulling her closer, until his body was pressed against hers, and their lips almost touching. The warmth of his breath brought nerve-endings tingling to life, just as his eyes caught her attention, and held it with resolve. "Because you're like winter sunshine," he whispered. "And, though there are days when fog keeps it hidden from view, for far longer than it should, there's no amount of wishing will clear it any quicker. But it's always worth the wait, my Amy… and so are you."

First Kiss

An unfamiliar and slightly awkward weight rests against my heart. Contentment and a sense of awe chase away the pain-filled uncertainty of recent hours.

I've waited so long for this moment. Years of patience and heartache, and recently, so many moments when I feared she wouldn't come to me, despite how I loved her, had connected with her, and craved her presence in my arms.

Now at last she's here—safe. My beautiful Agnes, bathed in summer sunshine, and bound to me in ways that enslave me.

The memory of another's death had hovered close... the recalled denial, and dark mourning, as terrifying as ever—but never forgotten.

Now, happiness consumes all other emotion.

Lowering my head, I surrender to temptation, my lips pressing against her soft skin in a tender caress. Our first kiss, filled with love and wonder. Breathing deep, I take her delicate scent inside me, revelling in the feel of her hair against my cheek, and the gentle breaths that puff from rosebud lips. So perfect... how can I *not* love her?

Soul-searching blue eyes blink up at me, filled with trust and, I like to think, a hint of curiosity about what our future holds.

"Everything I can possibly give you," I whisper, pride in her presence, here in my arms, and the need to remember everything as it is at this moment, warring with the urge to dream, to plan, and to set in place the safeguards that will protect her for all time.

"So, I'm ousted from your affections then?" a voice asks; it's tired, but not defeated, with a vein of deep satisfaction running through it, as rich as any gold seam. There's amusement too, at my apparently fickle heart.

Glancing up, I smile into the blue eyes I've loved for half my lifetime; the eyes that know me better than anyone else on Earth, who *see* me like no other. "Never, Babe, I'm sure I can handle the two of you."

Her expression is alight with tender mockery, backed by the knowledge that men are allowed these moments of weakness. Who would deny them that, when presented with everything they've dreamed of? Times of joy can overwhelm the strongest individual, but that doesn't make them truly weak—merely human.

"Just as well…" she whispers, the sound growing ever sleepier. "Because I'm sure Agnes will break your heart at some point." She waves a hand towards my newest love, held so reverently against my heart. "You adore her now, but that might not last. Are you ready for the rollercoaster ride? Are you ready to love her, even when she stares at you with tears and accusation in her eyes?"

My smile widens. "Are you trying to scare me away from her? There's no need for you to be jealous, you know."

Two pairs of blue eyes seem to laugh at my innocence now, but I don't care. This is *my* day—*our* day—and I couldn't be happier.

"She'll break your heart, Toby… just so long as you know," my first love whispers, her mouth curving to match the humour in her gaze.

I nod in agreement, unfazed by the challenge. "That goes without saying—it's the power every daughter has over her father… grey hairs and worry-lines are guaranteed."

My wife settles back against the pillows with a laugh. "So are nappy changes and sleepless nights."

"Ah, Amy," I whisper. "Let's not spoil the moment."

Beautiful Bravery

Agnes squirmed in her seat, eyes darting from ornate wood carving to solemn stone column. The pews, window ledges, pulpit and altar were swathed with opulent arrangements of greenery, interspersed with red holly berries and the large, starry blooms of poinsettia flowers.

The Church looked beautiful, decked out in its Christmas finery.

A gentle glow rose up from the tops of imposing, cream-white candles, each of them arranged into elegant groups. Their light flickered constantly, in an ongoing battle between heated flame and the cold draughts encircling the Church's interior.

Yet all this beauty made no impression on Agnes at all. None of it made up for the discomfort of hard wooden seats, or the soporific drone of the Vicar's voice.

Her discreet squirming morphed into fidgeting. How much longer did she have to sit here? She was beginning to feel cold; the sort of cold that seeps into your bones, and takes a hot water-bottle and being wrapped in a soft, thick duvet to get rid of. Shifting in her seat, trying to get comfortable, Agnes pulled in a lungful of cool air and experimented with how long she could hold it for before she burst at the seams. One, two, three… her foot tapped out the seconds on the wooden floorboards… forty-four, forty-five… no, that was it. She let the air go noisily and dragged in another long breath, ready to start again.

"Agnes!"

Looking up, she wasn't surprised to see the exasperation on her mother's face. "Sorry Mum," she whispered, and then clarified the need for entertainment. "I'm just *so* bored!"

Mum, who wasn't nearly as strict as Dad, smiled slightly and leant down in a conspiratorial manner. "I know, sweet-pea. Look, why don't you go see your friend, Tommy, for a while? You can give him his present."

At last; relief surged through Agnes. This was the green light she'd been waiting for. Nodding, she tried to communicate her thanks by being as quiet as she could, whilst squeezing through the tiny gap between the end of their pew and the wall.

Once free, she crept past the heavy Church door and across to the space behind the font, where Sunday school was usually held. Once there, she arranged herself, crossed legged on the floor, and squinted into the surrounding gloom.

There was no need for words. She could already see Tommy, sitting on one of the simple wooden chairs. He was watching her, silent as usual, his dark eyes gazing at her with something approaching surprise. That too wasn't unusual. Agnes smiled. Tommy was shy. She supposed it was because of his face—people could say such nasty things.

Didn't he know that it had never mattered to her?

Shaking her head, she regarded her friend as solemnly as he watched her. Next to her mum and dad, he was the most important person in her world; the only adult, apart from them, who accepted her exactly as she was, without comment, and without expectation.

Long moments passed. The staring continued. Until, finally, Agnes gave in. She reached into her coat pocket, and pulled out a folded piece of paper. Then she opened it up.

Her eyes flicked back and forth, between the paper in her hands, and Tommy. "I brought you a present," she whispered.

Not surprisingly, Tommy didn't reply. His poor, damaged face showing no hint as to whether he'd even heard her. Agnes waited for another heartbeat, and then placed the paper on the floor, right side up, and slid it towards him.

Slowly, Tommy leaned forward, his scarred hand reaching from the shadows, moments before his face cleared them. The candlelight softened his ravaged features, giving an inner glow to his dark eyes. She smiled in encouragement, pushing the paper a little closer to him. Tommy was beautiful to her, and so brave. He offered her all the freedom she would ever need; to be herself. It was hard not to hold her breath when he pulled the paper back towards him, into the semi-darkness. She watched as he scanned it, his eyes narrowed.

Would he like it? Would he mind?

The congregation had started to sing 'Silent Night', their voices filling the Church with reverent music, and Tommy's eyes suddenly widened, his mouth dropping open, into a softly rounded 'O'. The paper held the colourful lines of a naively drawn picture. It showed a family, with arms linked, and a Christmas tree beside them. Four figures, all with simple titles beneath: Mum, Dad, Me, Tommy.

When he looked up at her again, Agnes smiled with relief. He liked it, she was almost sure he did, but... why was he crying?

Had she gone too far? She'd only wanted to make him see himself as she did. He wasn't that old, and she thought of him as part of her family; the big brother she'd always wanted. She never had understood why he was alone, but had wanted him to understand that he didn't have to be.

Especially now, at Christmas; he deserved better than that. Something told her he'd *earned* better than that. He was beautiful, despite the scars, and so brave. Even if he did hide in the shadows, at least he was *here*, with the courage to let her be his friend.

"Thank you, Agnes."

The words were so softly spoken, she almost missed them. The chorus of 'Silent Night' swelled once more, drifting into their private space. A cold draught raised goose bumps along Agnes's arms, despite her coat, and she turned her head to see if the Church door had opened.

Almost immediately, there was a scraping noise, the distinctive sound of wood against hollow floorboards, and the thud of heavy boots walking quickly away. Whipping her head back round, Agnes blinked for a moment, slightly dizzy from the rapid movement.

The chair Tommy had been sitting in was empty.

She'd wondered when he'd leave. He made a habit of going quickly, without saying goodbye to her. It was as if he found being around other people too hard. She didn't mind though; Tommy was shy.

Agnes didn't go back to sit with her parents. Instead, she stayed where she was and stared up at the rectangle of white marble on the wall opposite. 'Silent Night' ended, and the Vicar bade his congregation a 'Merry Christmas' before retreating to his vestry. Her parents came to find her.

"Are you ready for home, sweet-pea?" Dad asked, crouching down beside her. His big arms reached out, scooping her up into a hug. Mum laughed, ruffling her blonde curls.

"Yes," Agnes said, burrowing her face into her dad's shoulder. She was starting to feel sleepy.

When she yawned, her dad smiled at her. "8.30pm is late for a six-year-old, especially one who's over-excited about Christmas Day," he said; more to his wife than his daughter.

"Tommy's gone," Agnes stated, her voice sleepily soft.

"He's probably on his way home, to bed—just like you," Dad soothed, raising an eyebrow towards Mum. "Did he like your present?"

Agnes's eyes were almost closed now, and she didn't feel like opening them again. All she could manage was a tired nod.

Carrying his now sleeping daughter towards the Church door, Toby Jewitt glanced around carefully before nodding over towards Tommy's chair. "It's over there," he whispered, shifting Agnes's weight in his arms.

"I see it," Amy said, bending to retrieve the drawing that was wedged between Tommy's chair and the wall.

She pocketed it, a thoughtful look crossing her face as she raised her eyes to the white marble plaque above them. It listed all those from their village, who had given their lives during the First World War. The name of Agnes's Great, Great Grandfather, Thomas Jewitt, was easy to spot.

"'Night, Tommy," Amy murmured, before turning to follow her husband and child.

From a darkened corner, Tommy watched them leave. For the first time in close to one hundred years, he felt at peace. And it was all down to one small girl, with angel-blonde curls and a heart as big as... Christmas.

Act of Remembrance

The scarlet poppy, which had started out so crisp, was looking decidedly crumpled. The edges of its petals curled inward, and splatter marks marred the inner surface, from when it had fallen, briefly, into a puddle.

Sighing, Agnes turned from the hallway mirror and plucked the poppy from her collar. She glanced towards the nearby bin, but thought better of it. Being thrown away was an inglorious end; however ephemeral the object.

Walking through to her study, she opened the bottom drawer of the desk, intending to toss the poppy inside. But a flash of red caught her eye. Surprised, she bent lower, moving sheets of scrap paper aside, until she revealed a whole pile of worse-for-wear poppies. There were nineteen in total; twenty with this year's addition.

"That's a lot of poppies," Agnes whispered, her heart contracting as she realised what else it meant. It was a lot of years, too: years of doing the same thing, without thought or variation. Years spent alone.

She'd been eighteen when her parents were killed in a traffic accident; old enough to take care of herself, but too young for the pain of loss, and the ensuing loneliness.

"So what do I do with a pile of old poppies?" she wondered out loud. Leaving them in a drawer seemed as bad as throwing them away.

She'd been on her way out. Maybe... Gathering up the poppies, this time into a plastic carrier-bag, Agnes found she had a new focus. It made a change from forcing herself to find ways of breaking up the weekends. Not an easy task, with no visitors, and no phone calls.

On reaching the village war memorial, Agnes regarded it solemnly. A plainly hewn cross, its only decoration was the names of the fallen; and wreathes of poppies. There was always at least one, but the number had multiplied since Remembrance Day.

Seeing the flaw in her half-formed plan—to find some way of leaving *her* poppies here, Agnes frowned. She had no way to secure them against the marble. Disappointed, she glanced about, hoping that inspiration would strike. It didn't...

Her gaze rested on the Church to her left, partially screened by yew trees. She'd always thought it a beautiful building, with its weathered stone walls, jewel-coloured windows and surprisingly intact lead work. A wrought iron arch marked the entrance, and a sweep of stone steps led to the graveyard that surrounded it. She remembered her mother spending hours there, wandering amongst the time-worn monoliths. With Agnes held firmly by the hand, she would point out the patterns created by yellow and green lichens, and trace reverent fingers across barely discernible inscriptions.

Agnes hadn't understood why she did it, and often said so, grumbling about having to tag along. But her mother's reply was always the same: "Can't you feel it,

Agnes—the love that's here? It never goes away. That's something you should always remember. When you love someone, it becomes a powerful legacy. Even when you're dead and gone, your memory lingers on."

Her mother had been right about that... Agnes knew it because she'd been loved by both her parents. Thinking of them now, she considered taking the poppies to *their* grave—but she'd already laid flowers there. Her eyes went to the Church again, as another idea began to form.

"What are you doing?" A male voice asked, making Agnes jump.

Turning to look over her shoulder, she saw a strangely familiar-looking man, leaning against one of the headstones behind her. "I'm planting remembrance poppies."

The man came closer, openly curious. "Why didn't you put them on the war memorial?"

"I forgot to bring something to tie them with," Agnes replied, getting up and dusting soil from her knees. "Anyway, there was already plenty there."

"So you decided to leave them for..." the man squinted at the name carved into the stone, and smiled. "Robert Mallory?"

"Well, him and a few others," Agnes agreed, waving a hand towards the graves. "My family has lived in this village for generations, so I've left some for my relatives too." She glanced back at Robert Mallory's grave. "Someone once told me that this place is filled with love so, after the relatives, I picked my favourite inscriptions and... well, it seemed like they *should* be remembered."

Grey-green eyes examined her closely, crinkling at the corners with humour. Like her, the man was past his first youth, but there was something about him, and Agnes rather liked those eyes.

He stretched out a hand. "I think you're right. I'm *Nick* Mallory, by the way, new to the area, and happily investigating my local ancestry. How's that for a coincidence?"

Agnes laughed, and took the hand he offered. "Pretty amazing. Makes me wonder what comes next. I'm Agnes Jewitt—lived here all my life and not planning to move."

"Pleased to meet you," Nick said, still holding her hand. Another smile curved his mouth. "As for what happens next, how does a walk to the coffee shop sound? Fancy being my official guide to village life?"

Something like happiness stirred inside her, stretching lazily. "Yes, why not?" Agnes agreed, allowing herself to be towed through the graveyard *again*. Not that she minded this time.

Angel Slides

It was scary-high, higher than she'd expected—which made no sense at all, when she hadn't expected any of it.

Yet here she was, standing with feet pressed against an invisible barrier, facing a drop that had her heart thumping so hard, she could have sworn it was trying to escape. This had to be a dream—that was the only explanation—and she wasn't going to think of another one, because the last thing she remembered was driving home, through a rainstorm that had challenged the windscreen wipers and forced everyone on the road to slow to a crawl.

But now, there was no car, no rain, and she was standing on the edge of a 'certain death' precipice. A perfect blue and white sky surrounded her, and a refreshing, light breeze set her long hair dancing. The sight of miles and miles of cloud was alternately obscured and revealed by the billowing strands.

It was a world patterned by sunlight and shadow.

Looking down, she blinked. Aside from the fear, confusion gripped her. Where was her business suit— plain but serviceable—and her shoes? She didn't recognise the shapeless, unadorned garment she was wearing now; not at all. It covered her from neck to foot in heavy, cream-coloured cotton, hanging in wide folds, down to a hem that stopped just-short of her bare feet—bare in every sense. There wasn't even the sheen of her customary pink nail varnish—which was strange.

She thought about what else was strange, and realised that the pain had gone. It was something she only vaguely remembered, but was sure had been real. She tried to focus on the details. Had it been the sort of pain that wore a person down, returning day after day until cheerful optimism is scoured from life, or had it been the pain of trauma; sharp, angry and unexpected?

"Your family loves you…"

She turned her head, shocked by the whispered words, trying to hear more. It was difficult to tell which direction they'd come from, and she had a feeling they hadn't been the first. The recollection of earlier words crept into her mind—whispered endearments that made her heart swell, and gentle reminiscence that brought a smile to her lips. The latter had meandered through her childhood, and reckless, teenage days, when intoxicating youth had outmanoeuvred sense. These were followed by days of responsibility, days of laughter, days of uncertainty, and days of love… And though she couldn't remember if everything the words said was true—the thought that she wasn't always a sensible woman filled her with relief. Life would be boring without a little mischief.

"You're a beautiful person—inside and out."

Smiling, she realised that, actually, she *was*—and was surprised when the thought felt odd. Perhaps it was something she didn't always believe? She wondered if she was the sort of person who usually questioned her worth, her appeal, her talents…

It seemed a bleak outlook to have. What would make her feel like that? Did she take her cue from others—is that how the people around her saw her? Apart from the memories the voice had triggered, and the muddled memory of the car journey, her mind seemed loathed to show her anything else.

"There is no one like you... no one."

Hmm... she wasn't sure she believed *that*.

The breeze was picking up, swaying her body, and suddenly she was even closer to that terrifying edge, with only the invisible barrier keeping her safe. She thought harder, determined to remember... grey-green eyes. She could remember grey-green eyes! Were they part of the dream too? She didn't think so—but why did it feel like they were the only things holding her steady?

"Because I want you back... we want you back."

It was as if the wind had fingers now. It pulled at the cloth covering her, inching her forwards with relentless determination. Her hair blocked her vision again, and her heart was beating so fast, she felt nauseous. Raising one hand, shocked at the effort such a simple movement took, she batted the strands from her line of sight—and froze.

A shaft of sunlight held her in its beam, sweeping over and past her. It highlighted the drop she now faced, and illuminated the tops of the clouds, before slicing cleanly through them.

The breeze became a gale... and the barrier disappeared.

She was falling, the scream that left her lips lost amidst the shriek of the wind. But then—she wasn't falling—not exactly. She was sliding... faster and faster; first through the damp, swirling, white-grey of the clouds, then through the crispness of a summer day. At least, that's what it felt like. Sunlight was spread out on either side of her, bright and iridescent, streaming downwards in a steep, flat plane, like a children's slide, but higher and faster than anything she'd seen before.

Terror left, in a whoosh of unexpected laughter, as joy spiralled upwards and outwards from somewhere deep inside. She felt—like an angel, flying through the air on a beam of light that slanted from the sky, down and over the countryside. It was a ride as wild as it was beautiful, as impossible as it was thrilling, and as familiar as it was new.

"And now you know… my bonny, curious, lass."

Her head jerked as the words returned, this time in a different voice; one she knew, and yet didn't. The ground was rushing up towards her at an alarming rate, the smudges of green and gold, brown and blue, taking on recognisable form; fields, hills, roadways and rivers. Panic began to overlay the pleasure. She didn't want to hear *that* voice—where was the other that had spoken to her?

With her mind spinning in circles, searching for the connections that evaded her, she felt her body begin to spin too. Around and around she went, dizzy from flashes of light and cloud, sky and land, until she closed her eyes against the confusing images. But now she didn't know which way was up or which way down, could no longer feel the laughter and joy…

"Come home."

It was the first voice, back again.

"I don't know *how*!" she shouted, tears of frustration, hot and useless, pushing against closed eyelids as she continued to spin, out of control. And then, suddenly, the force of the downward momentum slewed her onto her back, flipped her onto her front.

Descending on her stomach, harsh, panicked breaths tore their way from her lungs—and she began to fight, trying to slow her descent. Stretching out her arms and hands, she braced herself against the surface she sped along. Pain slashed across every part of her body, taking her last breath, and the sound of the whooshing wind became the hiss and click of something more sinister… something mechanical.

"I love you… come back to me."

"I'm trying!" she cried, instinctively pushing upwards, until she flipped herself onto her back again, and could attempt to sit up. If she could gain control, could just raise her head—or even open her eyes… surely that would help. Tears leaked from beneath her eyelids, running down her cheeks in a defeated, heated stream. She knew that there was a part of her that rebelled against looking. Her pace hadn't slackened, and she had no idea where she was. What if she opened her eyes, only to witness the end of her life as she crashed into the ground?

"I need you!"

The words were like a jolt of electricity, so filled with pain that her own dimmed and eased in comparison. With a groan, she fought to raise her eyelids—a superhuman effort…

She was looking into grey-green eyes—Nick's eyes.

"You had us worried, love," he whispered, stroking the hand that lay nearest to him. "But you're awake now, and you're going to get better. Do you hear me? You're going to get better."

Something told her he was right… he usually was. Hadn't their children bought him a t-shirt to that effect—something about 'to save time, let's assume I know everything'? A smile curved her lips, even though the pain was back, clawing its way through her body with annoying efficiency, and the mechanical hiss, beep and click of medical machinery had her head pounding. Nick said he'd sort that out... but she was too tired to listen any longer.

There was blue sky out the window, layered between white clouds. These, in-turn, were shot through with sunbeams. It was weeks since the traffic accident that had put Agnes in hospital. She'd almost suffered the same fate as her parents... but today she was going home.

With the formalities and paperwork seen to, her family crowded into the room. Nicole, her youngest daughter, was still at home, being cared for by her best friend, Jake. But Agnes would see her again soon, and Alice and Pippa, sixteen and eighteen respectively, were here with Nick—the children and husband she'd briefly, horrifyingly, forgotten.

Alice and Pippa picked up her bags, stuffed full of all the 'home comforts' that had gradually infiltrated her hospital room. Nick simply smiled, crossing over to where she stood by the window, and slipping his arms around her from behind, until she was cradled against him, with his chin on her shoulder.

"It's a beautiful day," she said. "The Angel Slides are stunning…"

She felt his laugh as much as heard it. "They are indeed. Your Grandad must have been a wise old bloke; I always did like his name for sunbeams."

She smiled. "We used to sit on the grass, staring up at them, and wonder what it would feel like to race down them. Grandad said it would be terrifying, but that didn't stop me wanting to try."

"It's nice that they're out, and the weather glorious for you coming home. As for wanting to ride on an Angel Slide... you always were a curious lass," Nick murmured.

It was her turn to laugh now, even as the final piece of the jigsaw fell into place. "That's what Grandad called me—his bonny, curious lass."

Glass Universe

He never grew tired of watching her—twirling and gliding, stomping and shaking, letting her hair down from that ridiculously tight clip, until it flowed around her in a tangle of bronze curls.

Alice closed her eyes, releasing a long breath as tension slowly dissolved from her body. Stretching tall, she raised her arms and threw back her head. The feel of her muscles, elongating and flexing, gave her a sense of power that was sadly lacking in the rest of her life. She imagined herself as a graceful dancer, poised in perfect form, on a single note of music, before allowing the rhythm to drive her onwards.

He wished she'd be like this more often. It wasn't right that a spirit as complex as hers was boxed within the confines of an unappreciative world. Her life was too rigid, too filled with duty and responsibility. *Her* gifts: wild imagination, and the ability to let her soul float and dip, like a leaf on a stream, were either ignored or ridiculed.

He'd watched over her for so long now, through the filter of glass and immeasurable distance… to him, the inability of others to see her clearly, had taken on the mantle of a wilful crime.

It amazed Alice how music could change her mood in an instant. It was almost organic, curling around her body and mind, urging her to do things she'd never dare in public. The hollow ring of leather on wood was like a percussion instrument, enhancing the moves of her body as she translated the notes into dance.

Living where she did, there was no one who understood her passion for Country music—but here, alone, in the refuge of her home, she could push back the furniture and throw the curtains wide, letting in rays of light, and the deserted garden views. Here, with a less-than-cultured voice filling the air with deeply accented beats, none of the little stuff mattered. Heck, none of the big stuff mattered either.

She could shake her imperfect body, stamp with abandon, and punch the air like someone half her age. And there was no need to worry how any of it made her look—because no one could see.

What was wrong with the people in her life? Couldn't they see what a treasure had sprouted up amongst them? His eyes caressed her as she moved, his fingers itching to hold her—safe—like a precious work of art created only for him. He imagined how she'd fit in his arms, how the pureness of her energy would cascaded across the jagged edges of his mind.

They'd been born so differently, but if he could reach out to her, just once, he *knew* they'd be a perfect match.

"Tonight, it's like, we never say goodbye…" Alice sang out loud, as she twirled across the floor, letting the cares of the workday fall from her shoulders. It made a

change that the words were by an English group, *The Shires*. Since the moment she'd downloaded their debut album, it had been playing on repeat; because she *loved* it—which was strange, really.

If she'd grown up in America, her obsession would have been more understandable, but here in rural England? Perhaps it was something to be laid at the feet of her childhood friends: two girls who'd travelled from the USA with their family, when their father was seconded to the UK. After all, it was definitely their fault that she had a fondness for Dr Seuss, and a taste for peanut butter and jam sandwiches.

He wished he could get closer. What was she thinking when she sang those words? How he wanted them to be true… What daydreams made her smile in that secretive way, as she swung her hips from side to side, and let her feet tap and shuffle their way across the floor— always in rhythm?

If he could only turn his head a little further, meet her eyes with his. No reflections and no misunderstandings.

He'd already lingered here for far too long, drawn to her so strongly it was as if their souls had already merged. Her presence was the only thing that mattered to him, bringing a sense of rightness and belonging that he'd given-up trying to understand. Did she even know how beautiful she was?

The light outside the windows dimmed, evening overwhelmed by night, but still the music swayed Alice's body. Truth be told, she enjoyed the magical feel of this time of day.

As the view of the garden became nothing more than a blank, featureless canvass, the windows around her were transformed into dark mirrors. Her own image, and the lights of her home, were reflected back at her; an eerie copy of reality.

The automatic mood-light on the sideboard flared to life, casting its aqua-tinted glow across Alice's most treasured possession. Instinctively, she turned on a graceful swirl, to face the only man in her life. Such a pity he was nothing more than a two dimensional work of art, however skilled his creator had been in producing something that *felt* three dimensional.

The fused-glass panel portrayed the body of a man, an outline of copper wire giving the appearance of pencil strokes, each one bringing to life the glorious possibilities of the male physique—albeit from behind—against a backdrop of planets and stars. The setting had always called to her, echoing her belief in a boundless universe.

She was looking at him now, he could feel it, with eyes he knew to be shimmering pools of green. How he ached to meet them with his own, to gaze at her as she hung in his arms, offering him all that she was—the woman, and the dancer.

How would it feel to have the sole care of such a bright entity, and to know she was there of her own free will? Impossible as the idea seemed, it stirred the passion that was never far from his thoughts. It tugged at his body whenever she was near, and he wondered if it was only his lack of courage that kept them apart.

Would they ever meet in *his* reality if he always faced away from her, failing to take that final step—in *their* dance?

Alice studied the glass panel as she moved to the music, suddenly aware that the man it pictured was someone she thought about on a regular basis, and not, surprisingly, only in terms of how perfect that back-view was.

No… she'd taken to building stories around him, of dreaming about meeting him in the real world. She'd join him on his cosmic journey, or watch in awe as he turned his head, to look at her with eyes full of knowledge—that she yearned to share.

Chuckling at such fanciful thoughts, she let the music take control once more, her steps flowing away from the panel and closer to those black, reflective windows. Yet even there she could still see him, his image mirrored back at her—inescapable. Tipping back her head, she tried to block him from her thoughts, arching her neck and closing her eyes. But her imagination refused to be denied, building the image of her perfect man on the backs of her lowered lids, until she finally gave in… and let him stay there.

Immediately, words of encouragement, whispered in a man's voice, slid into her mind. He praised her spirit and loving nature, accepting of the restless creativity that clawed at her office-bound existence.

The slide of her hair against her back became the touch of his fingers as they reverently smoothed across her warm, soft skin; and the tightness of wide elastic, encircling her waist, transformed into *his* arm. It curled about her, supporting her, as the music directed her emotions, and she gave her trust to a partner she couldn't see. In her mind's eye they moved across the floor in synchronicity, as one rather than two bodies, and she knew without doubt that to feel like this, a coming together of minds and bodies, was everything she craved in life.

His breath stalled in wonder. She was opening her mind at last, allowing the barriers between their worlds to fall like a curtain of silk. No longer was his gaze forced from her, and no longer was the image he saw a mere reflection.

For this brief, perfect time, he could be everything she needed, and she the focus of his world. It was enough—it had to be—though he still yearned to meet her eyes for real.

The music was ending; the warmth of his body pulling away from hers. But Alice recognised the scream of denial that welled inside her, the sharp need for it *never* to be over. Eyes flying wide, she searched for what was meant for *her*... until she could see only stars.

They never did find a body. Alice's house and contents passed to her Goddaughter, Emma, whom she hadn't seen in years. But despite this, Emma didn't feel it was right to sell her Godmother's property. Maybe if they'd known what happened to her... but that was a mystery that remained unsolved.

So instead, she moved in; a bitter-sweet experience. She and Alice had been close when Emma was little, and they'd shared a fascination for the beauty of art and music. The house was a place Emma remembered with affection, its contents full of childhood memories. Like the glass panel in the room Emma had chosen for her studio. Though her memory of it had been slightly different, she knew she'd enjoy creating her own works of art, in stained glass, beneath it.

With backs turned, and arms entwined, the couple's heads were angled towards an infinite universe. The woman's hair, a mass of copper-wire curls, cascaded across the gentle curves of a body filled with natural grace; the man's posture, curved around her, was all that was needed to show how he felt about the woman by his side. And unseen or not, it didn't take a genius to recognise one thing: Their eyes were filled with stars.

Love Languages

Love isn't about hearts and flowers. It doesn't have anything to do with chocolate or fancy meals out either. It took Pippa Mallory a long time to figure that out—four whole decades—and whilst she was at it, she realised that the saying 'Life begins at forty' should really be changed to: 'Life seems clearer at forty'.

Which came as a bit of a shock; she'd always thought that her life was everything she wanted it to be. Since her late teens, she'd believed that 'Mr Right' was a myth, and the only person she could rely on was herself—she'd done quite well at it, too. Of course, it helped that she possessed attributes (intelligence and a methodical outlook) that allowed her to excel in her job as a Personal Assistant, and over the years she'd earned enough money to finance a home, a car, and the occasional holiday. She was content—mostly—and she had no complaints with her chosen career. None at all...

At least, that's how it was, right up to the day of her BIG 4-0; the day she began to deconstruct her life.

It started with the birthday cake her colleagues arranged for her. Blowing out the candles, Pippa considered that it looked elegantly pretty—but when they cut into it, the sponge was dense, sickly sweet, and filled with a whipped concoction that was more e-numbers than *real* ingredients. It left her feeling strangely unsettled, even when she appreciated the sentiment behind it. Then there was a party with too much alcohol, and presents that consisted of vouchers for designer clothes shops and a trip to the beautician, despite the fact that she'd dropped hint after hint about book tokens... and the unsettled feeling got worse. Didn't the people around her know her better than that? Suddenly, she felt hollow. As if there was something important, something vital, missing from her life—she just wasn't sure what it was.

The day after her birthday, Pippa had two weeks' holiday. She'd considered going abroad, getting away from the English weather, and sunning herself on a foreign beach—September could be so unpredictable when it came to temperature and the number of fine days. But at the last minute, she couldn't bring herself to do it, and had decided to stay nearer to home.

So here she was, in front of a single-storey stone cottage in Northumberland, with rain slashing down at her from dark-grey skies and steadily soaking its way through her overly-optimistic cotton shirt. Grabbing her case from the boot of the car, she dashed towards the protection of the cottage.

Once inside, disbelief at her stupidity set in. What on earth had possessed her to come *here*? She could have been in Italy or Spain by now... relaxing in the sunshine, instead of shaking raindrops from her hair, and wandering gloomily between the tiny kitchen, a sitting room (with dining table pushed into one corner) and the cottage's only bedroom. There wasn't even an en-suite for heaven's sake.

She felt a little better after she'd heated up a tin of her favourite chicken soup and eaten it with some thickly-cut bread and butter. The kettle was duly put to good use, a cup of tea prepared, and carried back into the living room, where she drank it in front of the now roaring fire.

It had taken her a while to figure out where everything was, and to remind herself how to light a fire... but she'd got there. Only then did she sit back and take a good looked around. It wasn't so bad.

When she'd seen the pictures of the cottage online, something about its cosy proportions and furnishings had appealed to her; as if she'd seen it before—though she was fairly certain this was her first trip to Northumberland.

Still... there was *something* familiar here.

After her meal, she'd realised the cottage didn't come with a dishwasher, and wished she'd read the listing for the property more thoroughly; instead of relying on some less-than-reliable 'gut-feeling'. Now, sitting with her cup of tea, with only the crackling fire for company, she also wished that she'd thought to pick-up a cake for pudding. Something simple, that would have gone well with the tea, perhaps with the sharpness of citrus to cut through the taste of sweet sponge—a lemon cake, she decided, watching the flames lick their way between the logs. Then she wondered why she'd thought that, when she couldn't remember the last time she'd had lemon cake.

The flames were all along the wood now, dancing, frenetic and tall, as if trying to follow the path of the smoke as it rose in sedate tendrils, to disappear into the chimney above.

'Grandma baked lemon cake'. The thought popped into Pippa's head, expanding and gaining detail, even as surprise made her pause mid-tea-sip. She remembered how her grandmother had served it with butter, just like

the bread she'd had tonight... on blue and white china. Pippa's crockery at home was a triumph in understated design—plain white and serviceable—nothing like the fussy pattern that had covered the surface of Grandma's dinner service. It was years since she'd thought about it...

One thought led to another. As the tea in her cup diminished, Pippa found herself remembering the two-up, two-down cottage that had been her grandparent's home, with its steep stairs and lovingly tended garden. When she'd gone to stay with them, sometimes for two weeks during the summer, she remembered how very little had been shop-bought; probably because the cottage was so rural. Cakes, pies and bread had all been baked fresh; the vegetables came straight from the garden, with jams and pickles being used to preserve the excess; eggs were laid by the chickens they kept and even some of the meat was provided by the pigs they reared. Mental snapshots of her sitting on the kitchen floor, cutting old clothes into strips, which her grandmother had then threaded through the weave of a hessian sack, stretched on a frame—to make a rag rug, flowed from Pippa's subconscious, along with the memory of an old, black-painted kitchen range, where a small fire always seemed to be burning, its soothing crackle as much a part of the picture as the dog and cats gathered in front of it.

There were no designer clothes or trips to the beauticians back then.

A log shifted in the fire, sending a flurry of sparks up into the chimney before everything settled back, the glow from the underside of the wood seeming to pulse with every breath of up-draught. Pippa became mesmerised by the way the fire ate at the fuel, the underside of it blackened and cracked, with edges encrusted in thick, white ash. Reaching out, she grabbed the brass poker from its stand and moved the logs around, until pieces of charred wood fell through the bars of the grate and onto the tray below. Even as she watched them drop, her eyelids wanted to mimic the action. It had been a long drive, and the evening was progressing rapidly. She still didn't know what was missing from her life, but perhaps if she slept on it, she'd have more of an idea.

The bedroom was cold after the warmth of the living room, but the bed was soft, the quilt inviting, and the setting of the cottage peaceful enough to guarantee a good night's sleep.

She didn't wake until a cockerel, somewhere far too close to the cottage, began crowing in the early morning—the internet hadn't mentioned *that* either.

Breakfast was two boiled eggs and another slice of the loaf she'd brought with her. She hadn't thought to bring eggs, but when she'd gone to collect the milk, which she'd asked to be delivered each day, there'd been a basket beside it, filled with half-a-dozen eggs and the same number of apples—none of which looked like they'd come from the supermarket.

Cradling a cup of tea in her hands, and more casually dressed than she'd been in years, Pippa eyed the remaining eggs... and made plans for the day. It was years since she'd baked, though she used to be good at it. She knew the village possessed a small shop, and now seemed an excellent time to explore what it had to offer. Pulling on her coat and walking shoes, she borrowed the basket the eggs and apples had been in, and set off—a sense of purpose in her stride.

Thankfully, the weather had improved, blue sky and sunlight playing hide-and-seek amidst fluffy, grey and white clouds. A light breeze refreshed, without the chill of the day before, and the lack of rain felt like a blessing.

The shop was as tiny as she'd expected, with an interior that didn't look like it had changed much in the last thirty years. It was the sort of business where, she suspected, the customers knew one another, and deviations from the usual flow of village life were seized upon—and viewed with cautious interest. Wandering round the surprisingly well-stocked shelves, picking up ingredients she hadn't made use of in quite some time, Pippa didn't begrudge her entertainment value one bit. In fact, by the time she reached the counter, she'd already passed the time of day with five other customers, answered questions on where she came from, how long she was staying, and how she was finding her temporary home. The latter was perhaps not as glowing as they'd hoped, given that she hadn't yet been in Northumberland for a full twenty four hours.

The shopkeeper was blatantly inspecting Pippa's purchases as she tallied up the total on the till and placed them back in the borrowed basket.

"Baking session?" she asked, her blue eyes twinkling in a plump, rosy-cheeked face without a scrap of makeup on it. Not that she needed it. Pippa had guessed her age to be somewhere over fifty, a conclusion mainly drawn from the amount of silver in her hair.

"I'm going to give it a go," she agreed. "I haven't had time to do any for a while, but I used to find it relaxing and, as I'm on holiday, I thought I'd treat myself to a cake, maybe two, some biscuits and…" her eye was caught by a display of jams further along the counter, the handwritten sign in front of them announcing that it was homemade, and being sold in aid of Cancer research. She picked up a jar of the raspberry, handed it to the shopkeeper, and smiled. "Perhaps some jam tarts as well."

The woman beamed at her. "Your man won't stand a chance against goodies like that. Whatever you're after, I reckon it's yours."

"But…" Pippa realised her mistake as soon as the word was uttered—crafty indeed. Oh well, she supposed it wouldn't hurt to continue, and donate willingly to the gossip circuit. "I'm not married—which is probably why I haven't baked for a while. There isn't much point when it's just me. But I'm on holiday, so stuffing my face for a few days is almost obligatory."

The woman smiled and nodded. "Can't argue with that logic, and if you feel you've overdone it, you can always go for a walk. That'll be £12.78 please. By the way, if you *do* decide you want to stretch your legs, call in at the Pub round the corner—there's a stand near the bar, with free information about the best walks in the area."

"At the Pub?" Pippa queried. "I'm not sure I'd feel comfy going in there without buying a drink or something…"

Another customer, who'd been shamelessly eavesdropping, and making no attempt to hide the fact, piped up from her position by the fresh-produce shelves. "You'll find the same leaflets in the Church. Its open most days—just stick your head around the door, and you can't miss 'em. They're piled right by the hymn books."

"Aye, you're right, Mrs Oxley... I'd forgotten that," the shopkeeper confirmed, handing over Pippa's change and nodding her head in agreement.

Pippa smiled at them both and gathered up the basket before turning to leave. "Thanks, I'll remember that. If you see me around, striding energetically, you'll know I'm burning calories."

The two women laughed, and even waved to her as she passed back through the shop's doorway. *'What nice people...'* Pippa thought as she made her way back to the cottage.

She'd forgotten how flour could get *everywhere*, and generally did. Sugar, too... Pippa seemed to be constantly wiping and tidying, in between weighing and mixing. But the smell that emanated from the oven was, in her opinion, worth it. The sweet, slightly eggy aroma of sponge cake, with just a hint of lemon from the rind she'd grated into the mixture, wafted through the warm air, setting her taste buds tingling.

A cooling rack, already filled with ginger biscuits, sat on the kitchen work surface—tempting her—but right now, she needed to make a start on the lemon syrup. *If* she could remember the quantities, that is. Staring at the bags of icing and caster sugar, Pippa racked her brains for which one her grandmother had used... and then decided it really didn't matter. Icing sugar would dissolve quicker and soak straight into the sponge, but any un-dissolved caster sugar would sit in a satisfying, crunchy layer on the cake's surface. So caster it would be.

She'd used the rind of two lemons in the sponge mixture, and now set about squeezing their juice into a pan before adding what she *thought* looked to be the right quantity of sugar. Just as she began to heat these up, the timer went off for the cake. Easing it off the oven shelf, she tested its readiness with a skewer—pleased that the mechanics of baking were coming back to her so easily—and then proceeded to prick the surface of the cake all over with the same implement. She'd baked the cake in a loaf tin, lining it with tin foil that extended up and over the shorter edges—she could remember her grandmother telling her that this would allow the cake to be lifted out of the tin more easily, once completely cold.

The lemon juice and sugar had warmed through now. Whipping it off the hob, Pippa poured it over the cake, making sure it was drizzled across the entirety. That done, she started on a Victoria sponge, thankful that she'd remembered to buy extra eggs, and followed this by making pastry for the jam tarts. The Raspberry jam would go perfectly in both.

There was a sense of satisfaction in doing the last of the washing-up that evening. Watching the daylight fade as the sun dropped lower, Pippa felt content. She'd dined on beans-on-toast (something she hadn't eaten since her teens), followed by a generous slice of lemon cake, and a guiltily consumed jam tart. But really, it had seemed wrong to do anything less... baking was always at its best when still warm. She'd resisted the Victoria sponge and ginger biscuits though, having realised that her waistline could only take so much. A walk around the village was already planned, including a stop-off at the Church, to pick up one of the leaflets they'd told her about in the shop. It would help disperse a few of those extra calories.

The village streets were wonderfully quiet, adding to the sense of peace that had slowly settled over her. If asked, she'd swear that her breaths were deeper, her muscles more relaxed, and her heart that bit lighter. By the time she reached the Church's arched doorway, she was in exactly the right frame of mind to really *look* at the building. Reaching out her hand, she even let her fingers trace across the rough, stone walls, appreciating the tactile quality of a building material that had remained in place for hundreds of years.

Wrought iron, in the shape of a hollow, twisted circle, turned easily under her hand, allowing her to push open the heavy, arched, wooden door. She found it amazing that such a place was left unlocked in this day and age. Perhaps there was CCTV? She couldn't believe that theft or vandalism wasn't a concern. You only had to watch the news or read a newspaper to realise that there was very little respect left in the world; not even for places as beautiful and aged as this.

Stepping through the door, she glanced around at rows of pews, the pulpit, and beyond that, the altar. The latter, she wasn't surprised to see, was bare… except for a simple wooden cross.

It seemed as if this holiday was a time for revisiting memories—somewhere along the path of life, Pippa had stopped going to church, though there had been a time when she attended every week, and belonged to a choir. She smiled at the thought; remembering the heavy folds of a long, blue robe, overlaid by a crisp-white surplice. It had flowed around her with a faintly starched rustle as she walked down the aisle, in procession behind the adult choir members. Such a clear recollection… it could have been yesterday.

She spotted the leaflets that the shopkeeper and her customer had mentioned. Just as described, they were piled beside the hymn and service books. Reaching for one, she slid it into her coat pocket, her eyes drawn to the claret and gold spines of the hymn books. Looking around her, Pippa decided that it wouldn't harm anyone if she took a peek. Picking one up, she carried it to a pew about half-way down the church, where she could stand and admire the evening sun, slanting through stained glass, and reflecting off the brass lectern. Flicking through the hymn book pages, she found an old favourite: *Lord of all Hopefulness*. Another look around, just to check... and she began to sing the words into the silence, her voice a steady, clear, mezzo soprano. It was nice to know she could still do the hymn justice—right up until she heard the distinctive *click* of the Church's door-handle. A flip of the cover, and Pippa had the hymn book closed. She was almost at the end of the pew by the time the Church's latest visitor stepped through the doorway.

It was a woman, her slim figure dressed beautifully, in a bias-cut tweed skirt and tailored jacket, with a pale-blue blouse beneath, its scallop-edged collar perfectly framing a single-strand of pearls. '*She looks like a vicar's wife,*' Pippa thought. Even the woman's hair, blonde, and liberally shot-through with silver strands, gave the appearance of calm good-sense, whilst leaving her friendly smile and curious green eyes undiminished. '*And I think I like her already,*' Pippa decided.

She really needed to stop making gut-based assumptions.

Although, as it happened, this one wasn't far from the mark. The closer they got to each other, the more the woman's smile broadened, until they were standing only feet apart, smiling widely at each other.

"Hello," the woman said, extending a hand to shake Pippa's, "I'm Jemima, the Reverend Price's wife. So sorry to disturb you, my dear, I didn't realise there was anyone here. Please—if you need more time, I'll be happy to come back later." The look she sent Pippa was openly inquisitive.

"Hello, I'm Pippa Mallory," she volunteered, shaking the outstretched hand. "And, thank you for the offer, but I'm done. Actually, I only came in to pick up a local-walk leaflet, but I got distracted... it's a long time since I've been in a Church, and longer still since I got to sit and enjoy the sense of peace."

"And sing?" Jemima asked.

Pippa's cheeks grew hot.

"Oh, I'm sorry," Jemima rushed on, "I didn't mean to embarrass you. I really didn't know anyone was here. I'd come to lock-up and... well, I heard you singing when I reached the porch. You have a lovely voice, you know—I didn't want to interrupt—but then my conscience got the better of me, and I came in anyway. Who taught you to sing?"

Still uncomfortable, Pippa allowed Jemima to smooth over her embarrassment. She really shouldn't be so self-conscious. "My dad; he wasn't a professional singer or anything, but he's the sort of person who whistles and sings all day. I used to join in. Later on, our local vicar taught me—he doubled-up as the Church's choir master..." she trailed off, unsure whether Jemima had really wanted to hear all that.

"We have vacancies in *this* Church's choir," Jemima said, non-too subtle.

"Oh, but I'm only on holiday..." Pippa replied, surprised to find she was genuinely regretful. She'd only been in the village for one day, and already she felt at home here.

"Ah." Jemima nodded in understanding. "So, apart from the atmosphere, and impromptu hymn singing, did you get chance to appreciate anything else about St Andrew's?"

"No, I'm afraid not."

"Well then, as someone with the inside info, I think it's my duty to show you around… if you'd like me to?" Jemima offered. "We're lucky to have a thriving crafts group here in the village. The ladies there sew, knit, quilt, paint, flower arrange—you name it, they can do it. As a result, we have beautiful tapestry kneelers, each one created by a member of the village community, banners to display during services, and even a patchwork cope, made from old ball gowns and wedding dresses—my husband still wears that when he officiates at weddings."

Pippa smiled, her gaze dropping to the kneelers Jemima had mentioned. They were each as individual in design as the people who'd made them; village scenes, flowers and fruit, the more traditional ones depicting doves and crosses. "I think it's lovely that the residents of the village pull together like that, to look after a building that's part of their history. An expression of love… in whatever language they're most fluent."

When she looked back up, she saw that Jemima was staring at her with her mouth slightly open. The heat of yet another blush began to work its way up Pippa's neck. She was getting far too fanciful in her middle-age.

"Do you know… that's exactly right," Jemima murmured. "I hadn't thought of it like that before. I'm useless with any sort of needle, but I can bake. I suppose that's how I show *my* love and support; by baking cakes for fundraising and the after-service gatherings."

"I would imagine you do a lot more than that," Pippa pointed out.

Jemima smiled. "Well, according to David, I do have a wealth of other talents—like knowing when to give advice and when to listen. Not that I believed I had *any* talents before I married him... I was quite prepared to hide in his shadow. But I'm something of a feminist these days."

"You are?" Pippa asked, surprised.

"Absolutely." Jemima laughed. "Although, I wouldn't be shocked to find out that the way *I* view feminism isn't the same as everyone else. It's all about interpretation, isn't it, and choice? In fact, it was David who first showed me how strong I am—usually, by chucking me into situations where it was a case of sink or swim. I'm not saying that I could do *everything* as well as he does, just as I *know* he can't do everything as well as I can, but overall, we balance each other, as equals, and that's as it should be, don't you think?"

"To be honest... I have no idea," Pippa confessed. "That said, it sounds like the kind of relationship my parents have, and my grandparents *had*. And as I've always respected the strength of those partnerships, I guess I'll have to agree with you." Then something occurred to her. "You know, talking of love languages, and talents, there might be lots of different variations on those, but they all have one thing in common."

"Which is?"

Pippa shrugged. "Time... time to get to know each other and time to show we care, by whatever means we can. The ladies of the village do that with craft, you do it by baking and being there for anyone who needs you. I…"

"Yes?" Jemima asked, her voice gentle.

"I don't know," Pippa replied baldly. "Is organisation a skill that helps people? I suppose I could organise events, but that isn't as creative as I'd like to be. I used to sing all the time, I used to help my grandmother with her rag-rugs, I used to bake—but gradually all of that has stopped. I baked for the first time in years this afternoon."

"But you're missing the point; your talent for organisation made all of those things *better*," Jemima said. "Tell me, when you sang with your dad—why was that?"

"He said it helped him with his work."

"So it helped him to organise his thoughts, and tasks for the day?" Jemima prompted. When Pippa nodded, she smiled. "And what part of the rag-rugs were you in charge of?"

"Cutting the cloth into strips and handing Grandma the pieces as she worked."

"In other words, you were making sure she had a constant supply of fabric—and I'm guessing it had to be the right colour—so that your grandmother never had to stop what she was doing? That takes organisation, too. As for baking, I think that's a no-brainer. If you aren't organised, then the kitchen soon looks a complete mess. You *do* see what I'm getting at, don't you? There's more than one way to show you care—so long, as you rightly said, you're willing to donate the time."

Pippa said nothing for a few moments, turning Jemima's words over in her head. Then she looked up at the vicar's wife and grinned. "You know, you're not bad at this advice stuff. I think your David got a good deal for his parishioners when he married you."

Jemima laughed. "Can I have that in writing? I could photocopy it and make sure it's pinned up on every one of the parish notice boards."

"You've actually made me want to bake again," Pippa said. "I enjoyed it today, but thought of it as part of my holiday away from the *real* world—maybe I'll carry on with it though."

"And the singing, too?" Jemima pushed.

"Hmm, maybe; I could sing whilst I bake. It might help me organise my ingredients and oven-timings more efficiently," Pippa replied, with tongue firmly in cheek.

"You never know," Jemima agreed, nodding her head with mock solemnity. Then she happened to glance at her watch. "Good grief, where did the time go? David will think I've been kidnapped if I don't get back soon." She gave the Church a quick scan, before they both headed towards the door, flicking off the lights as they went. "You picked up one of the leaflets you were after?" Jemima asked as they passed through the arched doorway.

"Oh yes, I have one right here," Pippa replied, patting her coat pocket. She stood and watched as Jemima locked up the inner and outer doors before slipping the heavy, old fashioned keys into her own jacket pocket. "It was nice meeting you, Jemima. I hope we see each other before I leave." She took the hand that was held out to her, returning the slight squeeze of fingers; in silent acknowledgement of how much the other woman had made her think about her life. Maybe she hadn't found *exactly* what was missing, but it felt as if she might have the answer sooner rather than later—something that was largely down to this meeting.

"I hope so too," Jemima said. "We have a service at 10.45am tomorrow morning if you're interested? It would give you a chance to stretch those vocal cords again?"

The last, posed as a hopeful question, made Pippa smile. "I'll certainly think about it."

They parted at the lych gate, with its canopy of terracotta tiles and weathered oak beams. Jemima headed across the road, to the Victorian era vicarage, and Pippa turned to walk down the snicket that led back towards her cottage. Twilight was fast heading towards night time, triggering the lantern-shaped street lights to flicker into life. They patterned the shadows with circles of gold, their auras fading to near-silver at the edges, and this, coupled with the steady ring of her shoes on the flagstone path and a waft of sweet, floral fragrance—night scented stocks?—from nearby gardens, gave the journey an almost magical feel.

'*I actually feel, happy,*' she realised, as she unlocked the cottage's door and took off her outdoor clothes.

Padding through to the kitchen in her socks, she filled up the kettle ready for making a cup of tea. Her gaze rested on the tin that contained the Victoria sponge, and the basket that she'd used earlier. When the kettle clicked off, she poured the boiling water into her mug, and gave the tea bag time to mash. Thinking about it, she really didn't need *two* cakes, and if it hadn't been for whoever had left the eggs, she knew she wouldn't have thought about baking anything. So... maybe she should show them how much she'd appreciated the thought.

With her mug of tea now prepared and sitting on the kitchen work surface, Pippa made a decision, and went to find pen and paper.

Thank you for the apples and eggs, they were much appreciated. I put the eggs to good use, baking for the first time in years. Thoroughly enjoyed myself!

Please accept this cake in return, and thank you again for the thoughtful gift.

Pippa Mallory x

P.S. Could you return the tin a.s.a.p. as it belongs to the rental cottage.

Scanning the quickly composed note, she slid it into the tin with the cake and put it in the basket, placing both outside the cottage door.

Her sleep was even more deep and peaceful that night.

The next morning, being a Sunday, there was no milk waiting—but the basket was still there; minus the Victoria sponge. It now held another half-dozen eggs and a bunch of carrots with their fern-like greenery still attached. Along with her baking ingredients, she'd purchased a few things for meals at the shop, including a tray of cubed stewing steak, some potatoes and a stalk of broccoli. The carrots would go well with those. And maybe she'd bake again today... although, not until after she'd been to Church. She wanted the chance to see Jemima doing her 'vicar's wife' role, and the thought of giving her voice a work-out was tempting.

For a small village, the service was well attended. Pippa made sure that she was one of the last in, and slid into a pew towards the back. If Jemima and the two women in the shop were anything to go by, then any new face was likely to cause a stir—and she really didn't want a barrage of curious stares and whispered suppositions.

She would have succeeded in her bid for anonymity, if it hadn't been for Jemima. Spotting Pippa as she took her seat, she proceeded to wave and smile, until every head in the congregation turned to see who she was waving at. Feeling uncomfortable, Pippa returned the gesture half-heartedly, and hunched a little lower in her seat. It was a relief when the stares became fewer, or at least more covert. Only one little girl, who looked about six-years-old, refused to look anywhere else. She was a pretty little thing; big dark eyes and a mass of equally dark hair, but uncomfortable looking, in what was obviously her Sunday best. In the end, Pippa returned her stare, with a deliberately wide smile, and watched as she began to tug at the elegant sleeve of the tall, rather splendidly-built man standing beside her. He, thankfully in possession of good manners, didn't turn round. Instead, he slanted his head downwards, to whisper something in the girl's ear. Strangely fascinated by the interaction, Pippa couldn't help smiling again as his slightly too long, salt-and-pepper hair fell forwards, before being brushed back with an impatient hand.

Whatever he said though, it worked… up to a point. The little girl still couldn't resist the odd peep backwards, flashing Pippa shy smiles all the way through the service.

Not that she minded. In fact, it wasn't long before the remembered pattern of the service had her relaxing just as much as the baking session the day before, and she pushed the discomfort of being a social novelty to the back of her mind. It was a joy to be able to sing without a care, allowing the organ music to flow over her, the notes finding their echo in her voice. If a person could float with happiness, Pippa was almost there. Never mind the changeable weather—this holiday was exactly what she'd needed.

At the end of the service, she debated with herself whether it would be rude to leave. Would Jemima be upset? She wasn't sure she could be responsible for that… the woman was too nice. So she waited in a corner of the area being used for tea and coffee, accepting a cup from a lady swathed in a floral pinny, but refusing the slice of fruit loaf that was offered along with it.

"Pippa, so pleased you decided to come!"

How Jemima had managed to sneak up on her, Pippa had no idea, but quick reflexes were needed when she jumped, and had to save the cup as it sloshed tea over the rim and rattled on its saucer. Her "Hello, Jemima," came out on a breathless whisper.

"I could hear you singing from the front of the Church, dear. Such a lovely tone—it really is a pity you're only here for a couple of weeks," Jemima carried on, with just enough volume to inform everyone around them of Pippa's status of holiday maker. Narrowing her eyes, Pippa wondered why there was a spark of mischief in her new-friend's gaze. "By the way, dear, I'd like to introduce you to some friends of mine," Jemima said, turning Pippa to face the two people now standing directly behind her. "This is Mr Alexander Wright and his daughter Lisa."

They were also the people Pippa had noticed earlier; the man with salt-and-pepper hair, and the girl who'd been staring at her. "Is this the lady you were telling Daddy about, Mrs Price?" the little girl asked.

Dark eyes, filled with curiosity, met Pippa's, as the girl bounced up and down with supressed excitement. Her next words came as a surprise, though.

"You're the lady who baked us the *beuoootiful* cake. I wanted some for my breakfast, but Daddy says we have to wait until lunchtime. I don't see why. You wouldn't mind if I ate your cake for breakfast, would you?" she asked, staring up at Pippa with an overly innocent expression.

Instantly suspicious, Pippa peeped up at the man who was holding the girl's hand, but hadn't uttered a word. His expression of resigned amusement confirmed her conclusion. She was being played. "Actually, if your daddy says no to cake at breakfast, I'm afraid I'd say no to cake at breakfast, too."

Six-year-olds, apparently, still stuck out their bottom lip when they didn't get what they wanted. For a moment, the girl glared at her, but the temper quickly passed when she looked up at the man holding her hand. "That's what you said she'd say. How did you know?"

"Because your daddy knows everything, Lisa," Jemima interrupted, her smile as falsely innocent as the girl's had been. "Now, why don't we leave Pippa and your daddy to discuss what else they might like to know about each other?" And with that, she grabbed Lisa's hand and towed her off towards the tea and coffee table.

The man, watching with open amusement now, turned to address Pippa. "Well, that wasn't as subtle as the other matchmaking Jemima's tried on me. I'm sorry, Miss Mallory, I hope my daughter and friend didn't embarrass you too much?" He stuck out a hand. "I know we've been introduced already, after a fashion, but I think we should start again, don't you? I'm Alexander Wright, how do you do."

"Er, very well, thank you," Pippa replied, accepting the handshake. "And I'm Pippa Mallory. But can I ask: how did you know I was a Miss?"

Green eyes smiled at her from beneath the salt-and-pepper hair. "Well, I could say that, knowing Jemima's a vicar's wife, it was a safe assumption. But actually, as your temporary landlord, I have your details on my computer at home... on your application form for renting the cottage," he continued, when Pippa stared at him blankly.

"Oh... oh, yes, of course you do," she replied, pulling away the hand she'd left with him for far too long. "You're the person responsible for the eggs and produce, then?"

Alexander nodded. "We have an orchard, vegetable garden and hens at home—I like to share them with whoever rents the cottage. Sometimes it's appreciated, other times not so much." He looked at Pippa with enough admiration to curl her toes. "I have to say though, yours is the first cake we've received as part of the deal. Lisa was over the moon when we found it in the basket this morning."

Pippa blushed. "Oh, well, I'm glad she was pleased with it. I take it *you* don't bake then?"

"No, I'm afraid not. Her mother did though." He paused, the green eyes becoming inquisitive now. "I can see that you're far too polite to ask about our situation, Miss Mallory, but it's not a secret. Lisa is my adopted daughter. Her father was a close friend of mine, and I had the great honour of being her godfather before I became her father. Unfortunately, as a result of fast-track fatherhood, my level of domesticity probably isn't as pronounced as it should be, and as for my cookery skills… let's just say that they've never really had the opportunity to develop."

Not knowing quite what to say to this, Pippa nodded, in what she hoped was an understanding manner, muttered a quiet "I see," and took another sip of her rapidly cooling drink. Feeling better for it, she felt safe enough to add to the conversation. "I'm glad I have a chance to thank you in person, Mr Wright. I wasn't sure if it was the cottage owner or a friendly neighbour who was leaving the basket. Today's eggs will come in useful, too."

"Ooh, are you going to bake again?" Lisa's voice preceded her as she emerged from behind Alexander and took his hand. "Are you going to make another cake?" she asked.

Pippa couldn't help smiling at the hopeful face. "Actually, I was going to try a baked egg custard. My grandmother used to make one every Sunday tea, and I fancy having a try at it. Thanks to you and your dad, I think I have all the right ingredients."

"Do you have a recipe for it?" Lisa asked. "Because if you don't, we have lots of cookery books that used to belong to my mum; I'd let you borrow one."

"Oh," Pippa looked up at Alexander in time to see his smothered smile. "Well, actually, I do have a recipe—on here," she explained, taking out her phone and showing Lisa the cookery website she used.

Lisa's face fell. "Yes, that's very clever, but… are you *sure* you don't want to borrow Mum's cookery books? I could bring some round to the cottage this afternoon." She paused for a moment, before announcing, "I could even help you with the baking if you'd like. I'm sure I'll be good at it."

Alexander gave a funny sort of cough, which might have been a chuckle in disguise. Pippa looked at him helplessly. "I'd give up, if I were you, Miss Mallory," he murmured. "Unless, of course, you don't want any help?"

Boxed into an emotionally-charged corner, Pippa had only one way out. "Well, of *course* I need some help. If you're sure you don't mind, Lisa, I'd be very happy if you could come to the cottage later."

"Can I bring Daddy, too?" Lisa asked.

"Er... if you'd like?" Pippa said, aware that she'd all but squeaked the words.

Alexander looked as if he was in danger of choking now. But instead, he reached down and encircled Lisa's waist, picking her up in a single swift movement, until he had her wedged under one arm, giggling and kicking her legs. "I think that's enough railroading for one day, minx," he commented. "We'll leave Miss Mallory to recover her breath." Then he glanced at Pippa. "Would three o'clock be okay, for baked custard duty?"

Pippa nodded, wondering how on earth they'd got to this point, and watched father and daughter make their way first to Jemima, and then out the Church door.

"Well," she breathed, "that escalated quickly."

An arm landed around her shoulders, and her 'friend' gave her a quick hug. "You see, Pippa?" Jemima said, sounding far too triumphant for Pippa's peace of mind. She should have known there was no arguing with a Vicar's wife. "You take the time to make a little girl extremely happy, by organising a baking afternoon she'll treasure, and who knows what love language it will lead to! By the way, I hope you have enough food for tea; because I have a feeling there'll be three of you."

That's when Pippa gave up the fight. It seemed that she was exactly where fate had intended her to be. All she could do now was hold on, and wait to see where the journey took her. With any luck, she'd find that missing piece of her life along the way...

Bitter Lemonade

Soft, powdered cheeks; permed, blue-rinsed hair; more wrinkles than the skin on cold custard, when you disturb it with your spoon; watery grey eyes behind bifocal lenses; white, wiry whiskers sprouting from upper lip and rounded chin.

This is how Lisa remembered Granny Elger—a lady who'd marked her childhood with card games, laughter, and an experience that still had the power to make her shiver… over thirty years on.

She'd been eight when 'Granny' Elger, an elderly neighbour, but no actual relation, began to look after her (whenever her parents went out).

Where Lisa's home was a triumph of colour-coordinated interior design, and cutting edge technology, Granny Elger's was a time-capsule that showcased the tastes of past decades. It was filled with faded, ugly tapestries (on upholstery and curtains), and dark, Victorian furniture—passed down from one generation to the next. The window sills of every room held impressive displays of cacti and African violets, and there were enough crocheted doilies and antimacassars to cover a football pitch.

It was a world as foreign to Lisa as pasta was to her 'meat and two veg' father. And yet, she loved it.

So she'd been delighted when her mum (Step mum to be precise) and dad, on a particularly dreary summer's day, in a year she couldn't quite recall, had decided to spend some time at the local museums. Having voiced her disapproval of the idea, it had been arranged that Lisa would stay with Granny Elger until they got back.

She remembered watching as her mum knocked on Granny's front door, and how she'd waited patiently for the sound of that elderly person's fluffy-slippered shuffle. But when the door swung open, Lisa was inside like a flash, calling goodbye to her mum as she ran into the living room, where she immediately spotted a box, sitting on a chenille-covered table, with two chairs pulled close.

"So…" Granny said, eventually following behind, "You ready to get thrashed at 'snap', young lady?"

"Are you?" Lisa countered.

Granny shrugged. "Would you like a biscuit and some lemonade before we start—or do you want to wait a bit?"

Lisa licked her lips, as the inside of her mouth moistened. "Do you have any custard creams?" she asked.

Granny chuckled. "When have I not?" she asked. She had a point. Custard creams were her favourites too.

"Okay then," Lisa said, licking her lips again, as she imagined the buttery, crumbly texture, the smell of vanilla, and the sweet tasting filling.

When Granny Elger moved towards the kitchen, muttering to herself, Lisa began to get ready for their card game. There were a couple of newspapers and a magazine that needed moving from the table. One of the newspapers, a local one, was open at an article with the headline 'Doing The Gerbil Jive'. It seemed to be something about a birthday party going horribly wrong... but she couldn't be bothered to read it in full, so put the whole lot in the magazine rack that sat beside Granny Elger's fireside chair. Satisfied, Lisa delved into the box on the table—searching, until she pulled out her prize: a pack of tatty, but much loved cards. Dealing them out, she paused regularly to study them. Instead of the usual hearts, diamonds, clubs and spades, they featured black and white photos of cruise liners. Historical vessels: like the Britannic, Titanic and Olympic, right through to the Queen Mary and Queen Elizabeth. Before he died, Granny's husband had told her all about them. He'd known tons of stuff about ships.

"Here we are," Granny announced. She placed a tray on the table, next to the two piles of cards that Lisa had carefully counted out. On it was a blue and white plate, which Lisa already knew came from Holland, piled high with custard creams. There was also a matching cup and saucer, filled with steaming tea, and a glass of lemonade. The glass wasn't the usual sort: tall, with bands of pink. This one was shorter, fatter, and decorated with a rather startled looking pheasant. It seemed familiar...

Lisa won at snap, so they played again, all the while munching on custard creams. It wasn't until the end of the third game that she reached for her lemonade.

Taking a large mouthful, a strange, bitter taste coated her tongue, and she pulled a face. "Yuk. This tastes funny."

"Rubbish," Granny replied. "It's the same lemonade you always have."

Lisa wasn't so sure. She took another sip, and wrinkled her nose. "I think there's something grainy in here…" she said, peering into the glass suspiciously. There was a milky coloured ring, running around the inside of the rim.

"You're imagining things," Granny Elger insisted, waving a hand in dismissal, before shuffling the cards for the next round of snap and dealing them out. But Lisa had finally figured out where she'd seen the glass before.

She looked through the kitchen door, to where a pair of false teeth lay drying by the sink—and began to feel sick.

"Granny," she whispered, "is this the glass you usually soak your falsies in?"

Granny nodded, and smiled. "It was the only one I could find. Don't worry though, I rinsed it out," she said, laying down her first card.

Doing The Gerbil Jive

"It was gerbils," the policeman told Patricia Markham, reporter for the Giggleswick Times.

"Gerbils?" she said, casting her eye over the gathered guests, all of whom had been evicted from Albert Smith's 84th birthday party, and told to stand in the car park across the road. "How on earth could gerbils cause this much panic *and,*" she continued, waving a hand at where Albert himself stood, "reduce a grown man to tears?"

"Wouldn't you cry if your birthday party was crashed by a herd of gerbils?" the policeman asked.

Patricia didn't bother to answer him, too busy wondering if gerbils actually came in herds.

"Turns out the little bleeders had been missing for weeks," a female party-guest volunteered, "and of course... they'd been breeding for England," she said, taking a long pull on the cigarette she held.

Patricia's pencil flew across her notepad, even as she made sure the paper's photographer got the shot she'd need. The woman preened as the shutter clicked, turning to one side, so the bright-blue satin of her dress caught the light. Never mind the fact that its seams were under severe strain, and the tiny buttons down its front looked ready to become miniature, airborne missiles with each inhalation of smoke.

"Albert had no idea they'd been making themselves at home in his airing cupboard," the woman continued, obviously thrilled to be the centre of attention. "Heard they'd made a right mess of his sheets... completely shredded."

Patricia shook her head in amazement. "So... Mr Smith had an infestation of gerbils, which then attacked his guests?"

The woman in blue looked thoughtful. "I don't think attacked is exactly the right word. Did you know that gerbils are affectionate by nature?"

Puzzled by what appeared to be a conversational detour, Patricia looked at the policeman, who simply shrugged. "No..." she replied, "I didn't know that."

"Well they are... and they like their comforts, too; somewhere warm and snug to curl up in. And there were a lot of old men at this party... the sorts who aren't as careful as they should be when it comes to their appearance. You can imagine the confusion."

Patricia rubbed her throbbing forehead. "No... sorry... you've lost me. Whose confusion are we talking about—the guests' or the gerbils'?"

The woman gave a shout of laughter. "Both! Them gerbils were like ninjas. They landed on the old-blokes' knees and made straight for the family jewels. And to be fair, an open fly probably looked like the perfect hiding place, until..."

"Until what?" Patricia asked.

"Until the screaming started. I tell ya, them old fellas were jumping around the place like they were twenty again. Doubt they'd moved like that since the jive days. They didn't care where they were going either. First the buffet table went, then the cake stand...

and then some idiot called the police because of all the noise."

Patricia and the policeman were now staring at the woman in stupefied silence, but she merely gave them a wink and took another pull on her cigarette.

"And there was me, thinking only squirrels went for nuts," Patricia muttered.

Nicole's Happy Ending

In a whirl of movement, fingers fall from textured keys, and shock steals my breath. But only for a moment; my hands, captured gently, are raised to skin, where fingertips might read the words that, to me, will always be silent.

"Guess who."

This is a game I've played a thousand times; touch replacing sight. This is a face I know well.

First, I explore the hair-line, where short, surprisingly thick strands give way to my questing fingers. Softly curling by nature, there is no order to them—they carry the scent of his art: linseed oil and turpentine. I move to the skin below, so much firmer than my own. Thick eyebrows that twitch beneath my touch; lashes, deliberately batted, to tickle me; rounded cheekbones, one slightly out of line; and a nose of large proportions, sharply angled. I complete the circuit, skimming across the prickle of a jaw and chin, both in need of shaving, to press my fingers against the parallel lines of *his* lips, outlined by chamfered edges, stretched taught now, and deepening at the corners—in a smile.

Jake.

Beneath my touch, the warmth of his breath, scented with the sharp pepper-mint of toothpaste, combines with the movement of lips, teeth, and tongue to form yet more words. A request to leave my beloved Perkins brailler—for an hour or so—to turn my mind from the stories I give life, through paper and raised dots...

My heart beats faster, and I nod. His friendship is a pleasure that I do not take for granted, enriched by the years we've known each other. My parents have always told me that I should never allow the physical barriers to grow into mental ones, until they box me in and keep me a prisoner... I can do so much more than others would have me believe. And I have tried so hard to prove their theory right. No one will ever imprison *me*, Nicole Mallory, in a place where no sight, and no sound, can weaken my ambition. My creative mind has saved me from stagnation, but here, in Jake, I have the joy of a human connection, with someone I know values me—as a *forever* friend?

The feel of his arms, sweeping me high, is a surprise. My chest and throat vibrate with humour, until even my lips tremble. The body holding mine responds in kind.

A rhythmic jolt of motion, and the cool caress of a breeze, scented with the freshness of recent rain and underlying layers of sweetness. Then comes a downward swoop, its suddenness unsettling, and the arms around me slip away, leaving my back and legs cradled against leather, the smell of polish strong. Jake's hands take mine, pushing my fingers onto flat, cold metal; guiding me, until it slides across my body and into the waiting holder. I feel the jolt as it clips into place, and the tightness of the strip of satin webbing, holding me secure. More jostling; a hand patting mine briefly. My seat quakes with the vibrations from a powerful motor.

I wonder what riding in a car is like for others… those who can see the landscape and hear the world around them. For me, cocooned by dark silence, it's exhilarating—speed becomes a physical experience. My body tenses with each swerve, the rush of air through an open window sends my hair into chaos, until my scalp tingles with shiver-like sensation.

Jake always leaves the window open…

It's over too soon. But even as I mourn the slackening pace, I register the smell of salt in the air, and turn my hand, until my fingers grip Jake's. He's brought me to my favourite place—to *our* beach, where the wind often carries the smell of campfires and barbeques, and the sand cushions my frequent falls, allowing me to move without fear, to twirl and dance with the breeze… and Jake. Turning my head towards his unseen form, happiness curves my mouth. The tightening of his hand tells me he understands.

He pulls me from the car.

I untie my shoes, sliding my feet free, and placing them on the sand, delving my toes into its damp softness. Holding me close, Jake guides my steps… until sand is replaced by cloth. I stop, confused—but he urges me downwards, to sit on the cloth-covered beach. I feel him drop beside me, the sand shifting beneath his weight, and the cloth moving as he does. Capturing my hands, he raises them to his lips once more. "A picnic for my girl… because I know you're *always* hungry."

We've known each other for so long, grown together in ways others wouldn't understand… but Jake has never called me *'my* girl'. Does he mean it?

I try to ask, my hands shaping words, but he stills their movement, insisting on food first. He's brought all my favourites: Scotch eggs, deliciously savoury, bound up with breadcrumbs that feel rough against my tongue; hunks of rich, oak-matured cheddar atop crunchy, butter slathered bread rolls; crisp lettuce, slightly bitter, and sweet, juicy tomatoes; followed by lemon tart, bright in flavour, and citrus scented.

Replete at last, my questions return… until I feel Jake's hand on mine, lifting it, turning it, pressing a kiss to its palm.

Disbelief and unfurling hope hold me still. Until finally, I feel his lips on mine, and the words he forms against them:

"Be my girl…

Family Tree

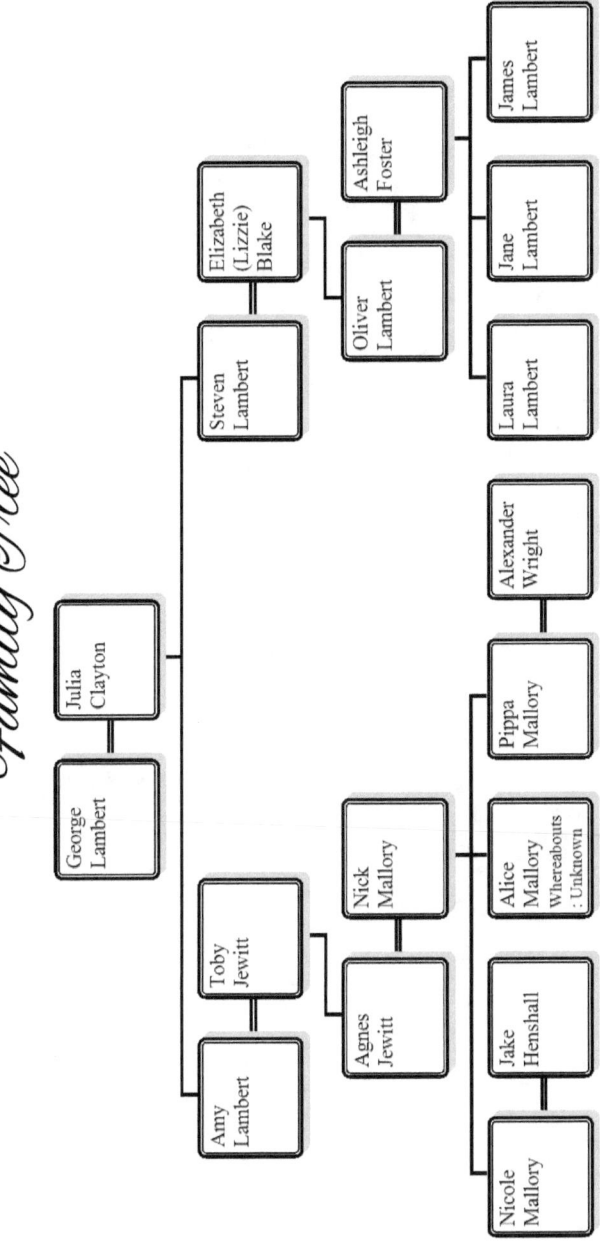

www.ingramcontent.com/pod-product-compliance
Lightning Source LLC
Chambersburg PA
CBHW050952120626
46552CB00001B/500